Get ready fo[illegible]

“There’s too much mon[illegible] More than a hundred million dollars has already been sunk into this production. The studio and the producers would shut down the film for sure if their insurance would cover the loss, but threats alone are not enough reason to cancel filming.”

“Oh, I see—somebody has to get hurt first. Great. Just great.”

My dad nodded. “Sad but true. Now, they’re coming to River Heights tomorrow night for the final week of filming. You can see why the mayor and the chief might be worried, even more than the studio or the insurers.”

“The town could face huge lawsuits if something happens here,” I said.

“Exactly. If whoever sent those emails means to carry out his threats, it’s going to happen right here in River Heights.”

“I see. Then if you’re going to hire someone undercover, you’ll want someone who knows this town inside out . . .”

NANCY DREW

girl detective™

#1 Without a Trace
#2 A Race Against Time
#3 False Notes
#4 High Risk
#5 Lights, Camera . . .
#6 Action!
#7 The Stolen Relic
#8 The Scarlet Macaw Scandal
#9 Secret of the Spa
#10 Uncivil Acts
#11 Riverboat Ruse
#12 Stop the Clock
#13 Trade Wind Danger
#14 Bad Times, Big Crimes
#15 Framed
#16 Dangerous Plays
#17 En Garde
#18 Pit of Vipers
#19 Orchid Thief
#20 Getting Burned
#21 Close Encounters
#22 Dressed to Steal
#23 Troubled Waters
#24 Murder on the Set

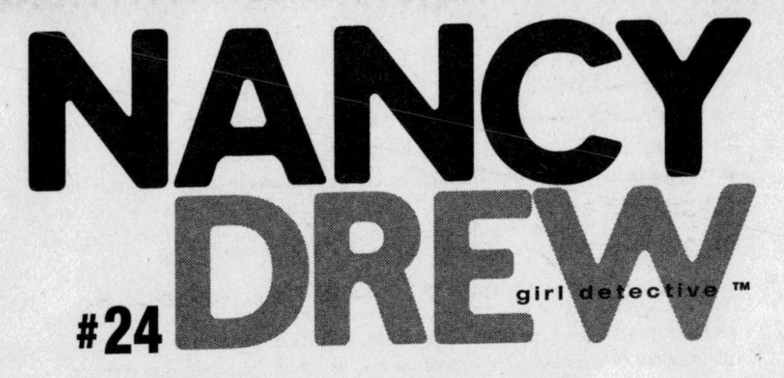

Murder on the Set

CAROLYN KEENE

Aladdin Paperbacks
New York London Toronto Sydney

ALADDIN PAPERBACKS
An imprint of Simon & Schuster Children's Publishing Division
1230 Avenue of the Americas, New York, NY 10020

Manufactured in the United States of America
First Aladdin Paperbacks edition May 2007
10 9 8 7 6 5 4 3 2 1
Library of Congress Control Number 2006929820
ISBN-13: 978-1-4169-3397-7
ISBN-10: 1-4169-3397-2

Contents

1

Opportunity Knocks

When your whole world gets turned upside down, it doesn't always happen in an instant. Sometimes it's just a little thing—an innocent moment that marks the beginning of an earthquake, a tsunami, a volcanic eruption.

This particular kind of moment happened to me, Nancy Drew, several months ago, but I'll always remember it like it was yesterday.

It was a quiet summer evening, and I was sitting in Einstein's Ice Cream Parlor with my two best friends in the world, Bess Marvin and George Fayne. Just three girls having fun, and ordering huge ice-cream concoctions and trying not to think about the consequences.

Bess had her newspaper spread out on the table,

and we were all sitting to one side, reading it with her. Not just any newspaper, but the one and only *Hollywood Gazette*.

"Honestly, I don't know what Brett sees in Fiona," Bess said, meaning, of course, Brett Harley and Fiona Gibson, two of the three hottest movie stars on the planet (the third being Brett's ex, Angelica Reeves).

"Maybe it's her big blue eyes, and her big red lips, and her"—I was about to say her fabulous blonde hair, but realized I was describing Bess to a tee.

"Her *what*?" Bess prodded.

"Never mind," I said.

"Y'know," George piped up, "if Brett's movies weren't all so trashy, we might care about which B-list star he was dating."

"Trashy? B-list?" Bess was outraged. I could see her always-rosy cheeks turning even rosier. "You have no idea what you're talking about. You call *Kill Me Deadly* trash? You call *Scimitar* trash? Have you even seen them?"

"I saw the trailers, and that was enough," George said, looking to see if the waiter was coming with our desserts.

Bess and George are first cousins, as well as best friends, but they couldn't be less alike if they were total strangers with no shared DNA. Bess is blonde, curvy, and, well, kind of short. At least when she's compared to me and George. She's good with a hammer and nails, can fix anything and find her way anywhere—but otherwise, she's a total girlie-girl.

George is taller than me (I'm 5'7", in case you were wondering). She's got short, dark hair, a talent for sports and computers, and a really high brow when movies are concerned.

"The only movies you like are in black and white or have subtitles," Bess shot back, turning the page of the paper.

George shot me a look and a half-smile, but she didn't answer. It was the beginning of summer—the weather was fine, life was good, and we were all in *way* too good a mood to let it be spoiled by something as trivial as an argument about Hollywood stars.

That wonderful feeling was about to change, really fast, but we didn't know it then. Ah, innocence . . .

The door of the ice cream parlor opened, and who should walk in but Dierdre Simmons, our worst nightmare at River Heights High. Each of us has more reasons to dislike Dierdre than we have fingers on our two hands.

"Ugh, why does she have to show up, just when we were having a good time?" George said.

"Maybe she won't see us," Bess said. "Then we won't have to say hello."

"Yoo-hoo!" Too late. Dierdre was waving and

weaving her way among the tables to where we were sitting. She had a copy of the *River Heights Bugle* in one hand.

"Hi Dee Dee," I said, using the nickname I know she hates. "How's it going?"

My little dig seemed to go right over her oblivious head. "I am so psyched!" she squealed, jumping up and down in front of us.

George, Bess, and I gave one another sideways glances. Had Dierdre really lost it completely or what?

"You do look . . . overheated," Bess commented. "What happened? Did Daddy buy you another new car?"

"Don't tell me you *don't know*!" Dierdre said. "I just assumed, when I saw you reading the *Hollywood Gazette*. . . . Oh. I see it's last week's. You really ought to spend the money on the new issue."

Bess's hands balled into fists. Dierdre is always telling people how cheap Bess is, and to be honest, it's no lie.

"Assumed what?" I asked.

"Well, it's even in the *River Heights Bugle*—Ned's paper. Surely you ought to read it every day, just out of loyalty, Nancy—especially considering he's your boyfriend."

You see how obnoxious she is? I could have kicked

her. Dierdre has had a crush on Ned Nickerson forever, and has always resented me for being his girlfriend.

"It's his *father* who's the publisher, so it's Mr. Nickerson's paper," I corrected her. "Ned just works there part-time—summers and between semesters."

"I know that," said Dierdre. "I buy the *Bugle* every day."

She clucked her tongue, brushed her curly black hair back, and flashed her big green eyes at us. "Well? Aren't you going to worm it out of me?"

"Worm *what* out of you?" Bess said.

Dierdre smiled. "Well—since you asked . . . Take a look at *this*!" She spread the *Bugle* out on top of Bess's *Gazette*.

Bess read the headline aloud, her eyes growing wide. "'Blockbuster movie to shoot scenes in River Heights. The new action/romance flick, *Love Me to Death*, marks director Gordon MacIntyre's big comeback, and stars Brett Harley and Fiona Gibson. . . .'"

Bess looked up from the paper and whispered, "Omigosh—they're coming *here*! To River Heights!" I honestly thought she was going to faint. It's a good thing she was sitting down.

"Read the next paragraph," Dierdre said. "It gets even better."

Bess was too excited to read, so I continued for

her. "'MacIntyre has put out a casting call for River Heights residents to audition for extras at a special casting session on July 9. The cast and crew of the movie arrives in town that night, and will be staying at the Hotel Metropole downtown. . . .'"

"Omigosh—I've got to be in it!" Bess cried out, so loud that half of Einstein's turned around to look.

"Fat chance," Dierdre said, looking Bess up and down and emphasizing the word *fat*.

Now, Bess is far from fat—she's curvy, and not a bit overweight. Well, no more than five pounds, anyway. But by this time, Dierdre had her totally psyched out.

"What, you think I'm fat?" Bess challenged her.

Dierdre let out a laugh and scooped up her copy of the *Bugle*. "Did *I* say that? Now you're putting words in my mouth." She folded the paper, tucked it back under her arm, and turned to go.

The waiter arrived at that exact moment with our gigantic ice-cream concoctions. "Enjoy your dessert!" Dierdre chirped, watching as Einstein's famous Chocolate Death Sundae was placed in front of Bess.

"Suddenly I'm not hungry," Bess said miserably. "I can't eat this. I'll look like a balloon at the casting session!"

"Good choice," Dierdre said. "But like I said—

fat chance." She turned on her heels and sashayed between the tables and right out the front door.

"The nerve of that . . . that . . ." George sputtered.

"We know exactly what you mean," I told her. "Don't we, Bess?"

"Go ahead and eat your ice cream, Bess," George encouraged her. "You look fine just the way you are: *Perfect*."

"If I eat this, I'm going to gain three pounds," Bess said, looking longingly at her Chocolate Death. "You eat it, George—you never gain any weight, no matter how much you pack it in."

It's true. George eats like an absolute pig and stays slim. I don't know how she does it, and neither does anybody else.

With a shrug and a satisfied smile, she moved Bess's tureen of tasty calories over to her own place setting—right next to the Mint Mountain she'd ordered for herself.

"Nan, do *you* think I'm too fat to be an extra?" Bess asked me.

"Not in the least. You look a lot like Fiona Gibson, in fact."

"You really think so?" Bess asked. "It's true, we are both natural blondes. . . ." Suddenly she was floating on air, ecstatic. That's so like Bess—if you don't like the mood she's in, just wait a minute.

"Totally," I said. Then, for some reason I'll never understand, I decided to lay it on a little thicker. "If your picture were next to Fiona's, people would think you were twin sisters."

I didn't mean *identical* twins, but that's how Bess took it. She checked herself out in the mirror, then looked at Fiona's picture in the paper. Then the mirror, then the picture. Mirror, picture . . .

"Bess," I said, "you really should go to that casting session. I'm sure they'll hire you."

"What makes you so sure?" Bess asked, suddenly worried. "I mean, everybody and their mother is going to show up for this casting call. And how many people do you think they're going to hire?"

"I have no clue," I said. "Maybe a couple hundred?"

"Out of twenty thousand people?" Bess shouted, again causing everyone in Einstein's to look over at us. "What are the odds of my getting cast?"

"One in two hundred," George said without even having to think. "One half of one percent."

"Thank you, math genius," Bess said. "See, Nancy? I'll never get cast. Dierdre's right!" Suddenly it was back to despair again.

"Bess, I *know* you can do it!" I said, massaging her obviously fragile ego.

"You've got to come to the casting session with me—both of you. We've all got to be in the movie together!" Bess said, crossing over the line into delusion.

"I have no interest in being in some cheesy movie," George said. "Forget it."

"Oh, get over yourself, George!" Bess said angrily. "This movie's going to be an all-time box office smash! Brett? Fiona? In the same picture? Can you say *ka-ching*?"

"Exactly," George said. "It's all about money. Yuck!"

"Oh, George, just come with me for moral support! I'll die if they don't pick me. I'll just expire!"

"You won't die," George said, "and no way am I going to go with you. I hate these big blockbuster action pictures. They have no soul, no heart, no brain. . . ."

"No being bored out of your gourd," Bess corrected her.

"Besides, from what I hear, extras do a lot of waiting around, and you know I can't stand that. And what if they give us a call time of 5 A.M.? You know I don't get up before nine, except for weddings and funerals."

Bess rolled her eyes, giving up on late-sleeping, impatient George. "How about you, Nancy?" she asked.

"Oh, not me—you know I get stage fright."

"Are you kidding?" Bess said, clucking her tongue, "you were fantastic in *Grease* last year!"

"I was in the chorus—in the *back* of the chorus."

"Well, that's like being an extra . . . kind of. Besides, being an extra doesn't take any talent at all! You just stand there and presto—you're in the movie."

"Umm . . ."

"Don't audition if you don't want to. Just come with me, please, please, please?"

To be honest, I would probably have begged off, but I could see Bess was really nervous, and really, really, really wanted to get cast in this movie. So I said, "Okay, if you want me to that badly . . ."

Bess screamed, jumped up in her seat, and reached over to hug me so tightly I thought she would snap my neck. For the third time in ten minutes, everyone in the restaurant turned to look at us.

"Bess, you're embarrassing us," George said. "Calm down."

Bess composed herself in a split second. "George," she said, "could you go over and buy a copy of the *Bugle* from the machine in front?"

Sighing, George got up, fished a quarter out of her jeans pocket, and went to the front, where the newspaper dispensers were. She and I both know there's no arguing with Bess.

"I *love* Brett Harley," Bess confided, grabbing my hand and squeezing it hard. "Nancy, if I get to meet him . . . if he shakes my hand . . . I'm never going to wash it again!"

"Eew," I said, removing my hand from hers. "Sounds gross."

She gave me a playful shove. "Now you're being cranky, just like George."

Speaking of George, she was just coming back with a copy of the *Bugle*—and with Ned trailing right behind her.

"Look who I picked up off the street," she said, sitting down and tossing the paper onto the opposite bench.

Ned reached over, gave me a kiss, then said, "Hi, girls. Mind if I sit down for a sec?"

He didn't really need an answer. He sat down facing us, and said, "Guess what?"

"Um . . . there's a movie going to be filmed in River Heights?" George took a wild guess.

"Bingo!" Ned said. "And my dad has assigned *me* to cover it for the paper. I'm going to be taking pictures." He held up the digital camera I'd gotten him for Christmas.

"Oh, that's so cool!" Bess said. "I'm going to be an extra." Suddenly she was already cast!

"Excellent!" Ned said. "You know, you could probably all get cast if you wanted to. They're casting seventy people or so."

Bess's face fell. "Only seventy?"

"Don't worry, Bess," I told her, taking her hand. "You'll get in. You'll see."

"I've just got to meet Brett!" Bess moaned. Then she turned to Ned. "Nancy's coming with me."

"I see," Ned said, surprised. "I didn't think you were into acting, Nan—or is it because you want to meet Brett, too? Should I be worried?"

"Don't be ridiculous. I'm not even auditioning. I'm just being a crutch for Bess."

"She's the best," said Bess, giving me a squeeze. "You're the best, Nancy."

"I know, I know," I said, digging into my ice cream with something less than excitement.

2

I Smell a Rat

We all went our separate ways, in our separate cars. What a terrible waste of gas, I said to myself as I steered my hybrid home to the house where I live with my dad and our housekeeper, Hannah (my mom died when I was three, and it's always been just us since then).

Even though it was still light out at a quarter to nine, the streetlights were already lit. As I pulled into the driveway I noticed that the light was on in my dad's ground-floor home office. It was late for him to be working, but I knew that as a top-tier lawyer, he sometimes had to take cases home with him.

I went inside, feeling like I'd been filled with liquid lead, and plopped down on the living room couch, kicking off my shoes. I was too bloated from all the ice cream I'd eaten to even reach for the TV remote.

In the quiet, I could hear my dad's voice coming from his office. The door must be open, I thought. That's unusual . . . .

Something about the tone of his voice caught my attention, sugar-addled as my brain was. Something worried . . . anxious . . . tense. I lay there, trying to pick out what he was saying, and found that I could only catch a word here and there.

You know what happened next. I got up oh-so quietly, then tiptoed over to the hallway, down the length of the long carpet, as close to his office as I needed to get and no closer (the wood creaks near his door, as I've learned from long snooping experience).

I could tell that he was on the phone. There were long silences, punctuated with him saying "Uh-huh . . . Oh, my . . . I see . . ." But then, he'd say something, like, "Now let me get this straight—" And that's when I smelled my first whiff of smoke. (You know what they say—where there's smoke, there's fire.)

"Let me make sure I understand," I heard him say. "This is not coming from you, but from Mayor Simmons, right? And she's afraid whoever's behind these threats may actually try to carry them out. . . . I understand completely. If something were to happen on the set while they were filming here, River Heights could be sued for big money—not to mention the damage to the town's reputation as a good place to do business . . ."

So there were threats that had something to do with the movie that was coming to town! Suddenly the idea of being an extra, and having an excuse to hang around on the set, began to seem much more appealing.

"Tell me more about the last film, where the girl was killed. What was she, a stuntwoman? . . . I see . . . But if it never resulted in actual charges being filed, the evidence must have been pretty weak. I'm amazed the studio is giving MacIntyre another shot after that. . . . Yeah, you're right, five years is a long time when you're in the movie business."

So there'd been a death on the set during filming of Gordon MacIntyre's last movie! Now that I thought back, I remembered the incident, which was briefly plastered all over the news before it was bumped by some other celebrity crime, I forget which . . . Five years *is* a long time.

"Well, I understand your concerns, Chief, believe me, I do. . . ."

So, it was Chief McGinnis my dad was talking to. The head honcho of the River Heights Police Department is not exactly my favorite crime fighter.

When he's not bungling a case, he's usually getting in the way of me solving one. And when I do, he's always there to take the credit. If you ask me, I think he's jealous of my success. (My dad thinks so too, by the way, so it's not just me.)

"Yes, yes, I totally agree. Having someone on the set is a good idea. Yes, you're right, it's got to be professionally done. It mustn't get out to the news media. . . . I'll see who I can dig up out of my files . . . no, I won't. I promise."

Meaning: Hire Nancy. Because, as Chief McGinnis loves to remind everyone and his brother, I am still technically an amateur. Even though I've got a better ratio of cases solved than he ever will.

"Bye, Chief. Speak to you soon." My dad hung up, and before I could tiptoe back out to the living room, he came barreling out of his office and almost knocked me over.

"Nancy!" he said, frowning. "What are you doing out here in the hallway? Snooping again?"

"Of course not, Dad, I—"

"I suppose you were just on your way to . . . where? The broom closet?"

"Um . . ."

"I thought not."

"Dad, I couldn't help overhearing, and well, you sounded worried, so I was worried about you, and—"

But instead of yelling at me, he put an arm around my shoulders and gave me a squeeze. "Well, since you already know what's up—"

"But I don't!" I insisted. "Really, I don't have a clue."

He shook his head, like he didn't believe a word I said. "Let's go have some tea in the kitchen," he suggested, which meant he was going to tell me anyway.

I followed him and plopped down onto a kitchen chair, still feeling bloated.

"You've probably heard there's a major motion picture coming to town to do some filming," he said as he filled the kettle. "The mayor wants someone undercover on the set. It seems there've been two threatening e-mails—one to Gordon MacIntyre, the film's director, and one to the film's leading man, Brett Harley."

"What did they say, exactly?"

"They threatened violence if the two men didn't quit the film."

"I see. Any way to trace them?"

"Not totally, but here's the thing. The e-mails came through a local server—meaning they originated in River Heights.'"

"You're kidding!"

"Some deranged fan, probably. I understand the stars of this movie are pretty famous."

"*Pretty* famous?" I shook my head in amazement, realizing he had no clue how huge Brett Harley and Fiona Gibson are. That's my dad for you. He never goes to the movies. On the rare occasions when he has a little free time, he usually spends it playing chess. "It helps me unwind," he always says, although I can't imagine how; chess is the bloodthirstiest game there is.

"Neither MacIntyre nor Harley is backing out—yet," my dad went on. "Apparently this movie is going to be a big box-office smash, and nobody wants to toss it overboard, because they'd lose out on their share of the profits."

"What I don't get is why Chief McGinnis called *you*," I said, getting right to the heart of the matter. "Why not just handle it with uniformed police?"

"The producers and the studio don't want dozens of police swarming everywhere, because it would attract bad press for them. So it has to be undercover. As for the chief, he doesn't want it to get out that the River Heights Police are 'spying' on the shoot. He figures if I hire a private investigator through my firm, the police force—and the town—are spared any embarrassment if things go wrong."

"Hmmm . . . seems like things are already going wrong," I said. "Why don't they just temporarily close down the film, until they catch whoever it is?"

"There's too much money at stake. More than a hundred million dollars has already been sunk into this production. The studio and the producers would shut down the film for sure if their insurance would cover the loss, but threats alone are not enough reason to cancel filming."

"Oh, I see—somebody has to get hurt first. Great. Just great."

My dad nodded. "Sad but true. Now, they're coming to River Heights tomorrow night for the final week of filming. You can see why the mayor and the chief might be worried, even more than the studio or the insurers."

"The town could face huge lawsuits if something happens here," I said.

"Exactly. If whoever sent those e-mails means to carry out his threats, it's going to happen right here in River Heights."

"Gee. Then if you're going to hire someone undercover, you'll want someone who knows this town inside out. . . ."

"Don't even think about it, Nancy."

I blinked, taken aback. How does my dad always know what I'm going to say next?

"Chief said he wanted me to hire a *professional.* That means, in McGinnis-speak, 'not you.'"

"But, Dad, I'm very professional!"

"Yes, you are, sweetheart. But *being* professional is different from being *a* professional."

"It is?"

"Of course."

"What's the difference?"

"Uh . . . er . . . look it up in the dictionary if you want to know. All I know is, McGinnis will have a fit if I give you the assignment."

"He doesn't have to know."

My dad, who had been pouring the tea, looked up at me, startled. "What did you say?"

"He doesn't have to know. Oh, and by the way, I happen to know the dictionary definition of 'professional.' It means 'someone who makes money at their job.'"

"Okay, smarty-pants," my dad said. "You want milk in your tea?"

"Please."

"So, what's this about McGinnis not having to know? Because, of course, he mustn't know . . . *if* I gave you the assignment, which I'm not doing . . . *yet* . . ."

"Dad, what if I *was* making money on this job, and it wasn't *you* who was paying me? I'd still be a professional, wouldn't I?"

"What are you suggesting?" he asked, handing me my tea and sitting down opposite me at the table.

"What if I got myself cast as an extra in the movie?"

He arched an eyebrow. "An extra?" he said, and the barest echo of a smile appeared at the corner of his mouth. "What a clever girl I have."

"It's the perfect cover, isn't it?"

"And an actress, too!"

"Hardly."

"Don't say that," he told me, giving me a look that was suddenly dead serious. "As I recall, you've acted your way out of some pretty dangerous situations."

"True. So, you don't mind me doing the job . . . unofficially?"

"Look, I'm going to have to hire somebody, to keep McGinnis happy. But if you want to snoop around as well, and you're on the set for a legitimate reason, who am I to object? As long as you don't put your safety or anyone else's at risk. Promise me you won't do that?"

Of course, nobody can guarantee anyone's safety when crime is concerned. That's pretty obvious, right? But my dad was asking me to be careful, and I knew it. So I promised, hoping it would be true.

It wasn't. Not by a long shot.

3

A Star Is Born

Notice how, in an instant, I'd bounced from "I'm just going along to give Bess a boost" to "I'm going to get cast in this movie no matter what!"

I showed up at Bess's the morning of the casting session decked out to the max, with my high-heeled leather boots, topped off with my best tank top and miniskirt, and, of course, my lucky sky-blue sweater.

Bess opened the door, took one look at me, and her jaw nearly hit the ground. "I thought you weren't interested in getting cast!" she said.

"I changed my mind. Is it that obvious?" I asked, wounded.

"You should have told me," she said. "I would have come over and picked out your outfit." My fashion taste is, well, not the best, which is why Bess is so great to have around at moments like these.

"Come in," she said, yanking me inside. "You need a total makeover, and we've only got fifteen minutes till George gets here."

"George? I thought she wasn't interested."

"She's not. But my car is in the shop, and hers isn't."

"What about *my* car? I drove it here, didn't I?"

"Nancy, you know you're the world's worst driver—and don't even bother to argue."

I wanted to argue, as a matter of fact. But I didn't, because it would have been useless. Somehow Bess and George have made their minds up about my perfectly decent driving, and there's no convincing them otherwise. It so happens that both my careless driving citations came when I was busy chasing criminals. Is it any wonder that I didn't see the ONE WAY or the NO U-TURN signs?

Bess dragged me upstairs to her bedroom and yanked off my sky-blue sweater. "Hey!" I complained. "That sweater is my good-luck charm!"

"Sorry, it's got to go, Nan. Here, try this one." Namely a hot-pink angora thingy.

So, okay, I let her dress me and redo my makeup. "You've got to blend it, Nan—like this." I admit it, I'm not a world-class fashion plate. I never had a mom around to teach me that stuff (Hannah doesn't even wear makeup). By the time Bess was done, I had to admit that I was an absolute knockout.

"There!" she said, happy with herself. "You're a masterpiece." A horn sounded outside. "And there's George, right on time. Let's go get ourselves cast in this movie!"

George was waiting inside her 1978 Lincoln Continental. It's got more than two hundred thousand miles on it, and all the leaks and rust and dents that go with old age. Funny how it was still running, while Bess was always, *always* repairing her cute new little import.

"Drive on, Jeeves," Bess said, sitting next to George while I settled into the back seat. We cruised down River Street toward the Mahoney Community Center, where the casting session was being held.

We hadn't gone far when the engine started to sputter. Before we knew it, the car stalled, and nothing George could do would get it going again. "Sorry," she said. "As soon as I've got enough saved up, I'm going to trade this in for something a little more reliable."

"Try to get something from the eighties, at least," Bess commented.

George tried the key once more, to no avail.

"Maybe you guys should call a cab?" she suggested.

"Nuts to that," Bess said, unbuckling her seatbelt. "By the time we did that, the casting session would be over!" She opened the car door and got out. "Pop the hood!"

George did as she was told, and Bess, the natural-born mechanic, peered down at the engine. Then she reached in and started fiddling with the hoses. "These are cracked and dry," she said. "You've got to get them replaced, George—this is a disgrace."

"Sorry," George said. "I just don't want to put any money into this bomb. Like I said, I'm getting rid of it soon."

"Not soon enough," Bess said, slamming down the hood and getting back into the car. "Got any wipes?" she asked, holding up her grease-stained hands.

"In the glove compartment," George said.

"Thank goodness," Bess said. "Did I get any on my outfit?"

"You're fine," George said, starting her up again. "You're gorgeous, okay?"

"You know, George, if you need to make money for a new car, you ought to come with us and try to get into the movie. The pay's pretty decent."

"No thanks," George said. "It's not worth the pain of working on a piece of trash."

"Who says it's going to be trash?" Bess asked.

"It's a Gordon MacIntyre film, isn't it? You know he's the king of sleaze."

"Who says?"

"Didn't someone actually die on the shoot of his last movie?" George asked. "Some stuntwoman or something?"

"That was an accident," Bess said. "No charges were ever filed against him."

"If I remember correctly, he got sued by her family," George went on. "They said it was all his fault because he didn't take enough safety precautions."

"Did they win the case?" I asked, suddenly curious. I remembered my dad saying something about it over the phone the night before. What was it he'd said . . . ?

"Who knows?" Bess said.

"I'll tell you one thing," George said. "He hasn't directed a movie since . . . not till this one."

"George, have you been reading my *Hollywood Gazettes*?" Bess wondered. "Quit gossiping and just drive. We're already late!"

We got rolling again, and were doing fine until we hit the corner of Bluff and River—total gridlock. The traffic was absolutely insane. I mean, River Heights has twenty-five thousand people, and it looked like every one of them was here.

"You see?" Bess said unhappily. "I told you it would be a mob scene. And they're only casting seventy people!"

"Don't worry," George said. "You guys are sure to get cast. Not everybody in this town looks like a supermodel, y'know."

Bess and I both laughed. We're not bad-looking, but supermodels? I don't think so.

"I think we'd better get out and walk," Bess said. "No offense, George, but I'm starting to sweat, and that can't be good." Even though it was still early in the day, it was blazing hot. The air-conditioning in George's car hadn't worked since the nineties.

"I'm trading this baby in real soon," George promised. "The AC's just too expensive to fix."

"Let us know when you get the new stretch limo, okay?" Bess said, getting out. "Thanks for the ride, cousin."

"Good luck!" George called after us. "I mean, break a leg!" That's what actors say instead of "good luck," so as not to jinx anything. I sure hoped it worked because I was starting to feel a bad attack of stage fright coming on.

The community center's gigantic gym was like Grand Central Station. A young woman with blonde hair piled up on top of her head stopped us at the door. "Girls to the left, guys to the right," she called out, trying to make herself heard over the noise, which was deafening. There had to be at least a thousand people in there.

We fought our way to the left, and joined a crowd of women bunched against one wall. An older lady with thick glasses and a silver wig that looked like a big boat on top of her head was saying, "Please line up for photos, ladies! Line up!"

We got on line—right behind none other than Dierdre Simmons. Just our luck.

"Hi, girls!" she chirped, giving us her best phony smile. "Gee, do you think you put on enough makeup?"

My hand automatically went to my cheek, checking. But Bess didn't even flinch. "At least we still look human," she shot back.

"Ouch!" Dierdre said, smirking. "Oh, and those outfits—they're so quaint. Did you get them at the Salvation Army?"

I thought Bess was going to lose it, so I put a hand on her shoulder, and said, "Never mind, Bess. To each her own."

Bess rolled her eyes and sighed, but didn't answer Dierdre back, and soon we were all getting our photos taken. Each of us was given a number matching the one on our photo. Then we were directed to sit in the bleachers that lined the long wall of the gym. We sat as far away from Dierdre as we could get.

"I can't stand that girl," Bess muttered. "Who does she think she is? Just because her father is the head of the country club. . . ."

"Who cares?" I said. "I just hope we get cast."

"Ooo, me too!" She gave my hand a squeeze.

Just then, a murmur went up from the crowd as a man entered the gym. I thought he looked familiar, and Bess confirmed it.

"That's Gordon MacIntyre!" she screamed in my ear, then started jumping up and down.

It wasn't just her, either. Half the girls surrounding us were doing the same thing, making the bleachers bounce and rattle. I could just see them collapsing under all the stress.

Gordon MacIntyre, the film's director, had long, dark hair that flowed down over his broad, manly shoulders. He was about 6'3", ruggedly handsome, and dressed in denim and cowboy boots. He had a moustache and goatee, and was just about the handsomest guy I'd ever seen.

"Wow," I said, my voice drowned out by the commotion in the stands. "He should be in front of the camera, not behind it."

"What?" Bess shouted at me.

"Nothing." I watched the blonde woman who'd greeted us go up and give Gordon a kiss and a squeeze.

I could tell from all the way across the gym that she was in love with him. Well, who could blame her?

He had a megaphone in one hand, and now raised it to his lips. "Attention, everybody!" his voice blasted out.

The crowd settled down slowly. "Thank you all for coming, and what a great turnout—I love you, River Heights!"

That got everyone going, and the whole room exploded in cheers. He motioned for silence, and when he had it, he continued. "We're going to go over these photos and start calling out numbers. If your number is called out, please see Tina. Tina, wave to the people." The blonde waved to us, beaming. "Tina's my assistant director, and if your number is called, you'll report to her. And now, here's Silvia Trout, our casting director for extras."

He handed the megaphone to the older lady with the bad wig and the thick glasses, who was standing at a long table with all of our photos displayed on it. "I'm going to start calling numbers now," she said. "If you hear your number, you have been selected to be an extra. Please remain where you are until we've finished calling numbers. All right, here we go . . . thirty-five . . . seventy-five . . . one fourteen . . . one thirty . . . one fifty-six . . . one sixty-five . . ."

"What number are you?" Bess asked me.

I checked my ticket. "Six fifty-four," I said.

"I'm six fifty-three . . . and Dierdre must be six fifty-two."

"Will you forget about her?" I said. "She's just a jerk. Pay no attention to—"

" . . . Six fifty-two . . ."

Dierdre, seated to our left, jumped to her feet and screamed. "Yes! Yes! I can't believe I got in!" she squealed.

"Pipe down," I told her. "I can't hear the numbers being called!"

"They said to remain seated," Bess reminded her.

"Oh, shut up. You're just jealous," Dierdre shot back, and proceeded to make her way down to the gym floor, where Sylvia Trout was still calling out numbers.

" . . . Six fifty-eight . . . six sixty-seven . . ."

"They skipped over us," Bess said, slowly sitting down. "We're not going to get picked. I can't believe it."

"Don't say that," I said, sitting down next to her. "You don't know that. She might go through the numbers again."

"Yeah, right," Bess said, resting her chin in her hands. "I'm sure."

"Eight thirty-two . . . eight fifty-six . . ."

I tried to count how many people had already

been picked. It looked like there were at least fifty people crowding around Tina, the assistant director, waving their numbered tickets.

Maybe Bess was right. Maybe we weren't going to make the cut.

Poor Bess. I wanted to throw my arms around her and let her cry on my shoulder. I could see how much this meant to her. I mean, I wanted to get into the movie, so I could investigate the threats, but for her, this was the opportunity of a lifetime.

I *know* Bess. I was sure she'd been fantasizing about "getting discovered" while on the movie set. In her dreams, Gordon MacIntyre would come up to her and ask her to star in the picture in Fiona's place. Then Brett would fall in love with her and forget all about Fiona.

". . . Nine fifty-three . . . nine eighty-five . . . and, that's it." Sylvia Trout handed the megaphone to Gordon.

"Casting session is over!" he called. "Anyone who did not hear their number called, please exit the facility at this time. Those of you whose numbers were called, please take a seat in the bleachers. We'll be handing you release forms to sign and giving you a call time and location for tomorrow."

Bess looked totally crushed. Her chin was trembling, and her eyes were tearing up fast.

Then something suddenly occurred to me. "You know what?" I said. "Maybe she *did* call out our numbers, but we just didn't hear it because Dierdre was screaming so loudly."

Bess blinked back her tears and turned to me, suddenly hopeful. "You know, you're right!" she said. "That little witch. She has the most annoying voice, doesn't she?"

"Totally. And she uses it at all the wrong times, to say all the worst things."

"We should go down there and check to see if they called us," Bess said, whipping out her compact mirror and dabbing at her mascara with a tissue. "Do I look all right?" she asked.

"Perfect," I assured her.

We made our way down to the gym floor and over to Sylvia's vicinity, to see what we could find out.

"Excuse me," I asked Sylvia. "I have a question—"

"Have we called your number?" she interrupted.

"Um, not yet, but—"

"The casting session is over, sweetheart. Please exit the facility, immediately."

"But—"

Too late. She'd already turned away from me to confer with Gordon MacIntyre and Tina.

I followed Bess out the doors and into the heat of the day. "That's it," said Bess. "My life is over. Dierdre

Shannon got cast, and I didn't. I can't believe it. This is so unfair!"

I looked around for George's car. It was nowhere in sight. "What time is she picking us up?"

Bess dabbed at her eyes. "Noon. What time is it?"

"Noon. I don't see her, though. Want to walk?"

"In this heat? Are you insane?"

So we sat there on the steps of the center, waiting. After a few minutes, the door opened behind us, and the people who'd been chosen as extras started to file out. Dierdre was among them. She spotted us and came over.

"Did you get cast?" she asked us, knowing full well we hadn't been.

"That woman Sylvia is obviously blind," Bess said. "Did you see those glasses of hers? If she could see herself in the mirror, she'd get a new wig, don't you think?"

"I think you're so mean!" Dierdre replied. "And just because she didn't pick you."

I thought Bess was about to go off on Dierdre, so I put a restraining hand on her arm. "Let her talk," I told her. "Who cares what she says, anyway?"

"Sore losers," Dierdre muttered.

The center's doors opened, and out came Sylvia Trout herself, deep in conversation with Tina. It was more like an argument.

"I *told* you Gordon needed a stand-in for her!" Tina was saying. "How do you let all these other people go without checking?"

"I thought we could use one of the extras," Sylvia explained.

"And save a little money?" Tina shot back. "Now we'll have to have a whole other casting session!"

"It's not *my* fault he didn't like any of the ones we picked."

"Gordon's very particular. She's got to look just like Fiona."

Bess grabbed my arm. "Did you hear that?" she whispered in my ear. "They're still looking for a stand-in for Fiona Gibson! My identical twin!"

She stood up, checked her makeup again, then swirled around to present herself to Tina and Sylvia.

But Dierdre had beaten her to it. "Excuse me," she said, "I couldn't help overhearing. I could easily be Fiona's stand-in if you like."

Tina snorted. "You? Weren't you already cast as an extra?"

"Yes, but—"

"If Gordon had wanted to use you, he would have pulled your picture."

"*I* wasn't cast as an extra!" Bess said, stepping forward. "So I'm available—and I do look a *little* like Fiona, don't you think?"

Sylvia and Tina checked Bess out while Dierdre looked on, steaming. "What do you think?" Sylvia asked.

Tina made a face. "There's a definite resemblance," she said. "But stand-ins have to be the right height—Fiona's five foot seven." Tina looked down at Bess, who was at least six inches shorter than her. "Are you five foot seven? You don't look it."

Bess is 5'2", in case you were wondering. But Tina didn't have to be so cold about it. Bess was feeling small enough as it was. Anyone with half a heart could tell that.

"How tall are you?"

"Five foot four," Bess said, lying like a rug.

"Too short," Tina said. "Besides, you don't have quite the right look."

"Not the right look?" Bess gasped. "We're dead ringers for each other! I'm practically her identical twin! Is everyone around here blind? I mean, we're both blondes, for starters!"

"Not anymore," Tina said flatly. "In this movie, Fiona's a redhead." She looked up and saw me sitting there. "Like her."

She walked down the three steps to where I was. At the same time, I stood up. "Were you at the session this morning?" she asked me.

"Uh-huh," I said.

"I guess I didn't pick up from your picture that you had red hair," Tina said. "How tall are you?"

"Um . . . five foot seven?" I said guiltily.

"Sylvia, is Gordon still here? I want him to see this one. Don't move," she told me.

Sylvia went back inside. A moment later she reemerged with Gordon MacIntyre himself. He came down the stairs, passing Bess and Dierdre without even looking at them. He stared at me long and hard, looking me up and down. I have to tell you, he had gorgeous eyes—blue-green with yellow zigzags all around the pupils. They were like jewels, and they kind of hypnotized me, just for a second.

He fiddled with my hair, fluffing it out as if I was a mannequin. "What's your name?" he asked.

"Um, Nancy Drew?" I said in a shaky voice that made me feel stupid. I'm sure I blushed beet red.

"Perfect," he said, turning to Sylvia. "Book her. We've got our stand-in for Fiona." With that, he bounded down the stairs, followed closely by Tina, who chased him around like she was his lapdog.

Sylvia was looking at me through her coke-bottle glasses, trying to make out whether I really looked enough like Fiona to be her double. "Do you know what a stand-in does, honey?" she asked me.

"Um, stands in?" I said stupidly.

Sylvia sighed, and made a disgusted face. "Just show

up with the extras at six a.m. tomorrow. The bus will be right outside this building."

"Bus?"

"Just be there."

She handed me a yellow slip to sign. It was a release form, saying I wouldn't sue the company if anything happened to me on the job. "Sign," she ordered.

I looked over at Bess, who was staring at me in horror. Dierdre had a look of pure fury on her face. But what could I do? This was my chance to be on the set, and, possibly, prevent a terrible crime!

I signed. Sylvia took the paper and said, "See you tomorrow." Then she headed down the steps and across the street.

I stood there, holding my copy of the release form in my hand, and turned to Bess. "Bess, I—"

"Tell me this is not happening," she said, staring at me as if she'd never really seen me before. "Omigosh—I've created a monster—I can't believe *I'm* the one who convinced you to come, and got you all dressed up—made up and everything—and now *you're* Fiona's stand-in! How could you do this to me, Nancy? I thought you were my best friend!"

"I *am*!" I called after her because by this time, Bess was running away from me, down the steps, and onto River Avenue, crying her eyes out.

"You creep," Dierdre muttered, still staring at me. "Some friend you are."

"But—"

"I wouldn't blame Bess if she never spoke to you again."

Whereas Bess had been hurt, Dierdre was bitter. "And don't think you're so innocent, either, Nancy. I'm sure they would have picked me over Bess if you hadn't been there, flashing that red hair of yours. You know it's from a bottle."

"It's not!" I said truthfully.

"And since when are you five foot seven?"

"Since I was fifteen."

"Is that so? Well, you watch me cut you down to size, Nancy Drew. I'm not taking this lying down. You haven't heard the last of me—not by a long shot."

As I watched her go, I kept folding my release form until it was a tiny, thick square. I was worried about Dierdre's threats, for sure, but I was even more worried about Bess. Would I ever be able to patch things up with my old friend?

4

Troubled Waters

As I was standing there on the steps of the center, I saw George's old Lincoln huffing and puffing down Bluff Street toward me, trailing blue smoke. I waved, and George slowed down. But just as I was about to run down the stairs and get in—and beg Bess to forgive me—the car sped up again, and kept on going.

I could see Bess sitting in the passenger seat. It didn't take a genius to figure out that she'd told George to keep driving and leave me there.

Okay, I could understand why she would do that. I'd hurt her feelings terribly. But I wasn't sure it was a good idea to tell her about my real reason for taking the job. Not yet, anyway. After all, it might turn out to be nothing, and then Bess would think I'd given her a lame excuse.

I took out my cell phone and called Ned. "Do you want to meet for lunch?" I asked him. "I'm at the center downtown. Bess and George just took off without me."

"I'd love to," Ned replied. "Give me five minutes."

The offices of the *River Heights Bugle* were only two blocks away. Ned came without his car, slipped a hand around my arm, and kissed me. I closed my eyes to kiss him back—and Gordon MacIntyre's face flashed into my mind. I guess I must have flinched or pulled back a little, because he noticed right away.

"What's the matter?"

"Nothing. Nothing at all," I insisted. "In fact, I just got cast in the movie!"

"You did? I thought you weren't even going to try out."

"I changed my mind," I said, not mentioning my reasons to him either.

"Well, that's fine by me," he said cheerfully as we walked down Bluff toward the Moonbeam Diner, one of our favorite places to eat. It's one of those old diners that was originally a train car, and it looks right out over the bluffs toward the river. Cheap, too. "I'm sure we'll be able to hang out together some—after all, I'm covering it for the paper, so I'll be allowed on the set, or at least pretty near it."

"I don't know about that," I said. "I think they're

going to keep the press far away, because they're expecting a mob of paparazzi."

Ned smiled his wonderful, crooked smile. "Ah, yes, but I'm with the local paper—the hometown boy," he said. "I think Chief McGinnis will make an exception in my case."

We took a table and ordered sandwiches. "So as I was saying, you'll have lots of time to hang out," Ned said. "Extras wait around for hours at a time in between shots."

"They do?"

"Uh-huh."

"That's good," I said. "Except I'm not an extra."

"What?"

"I'm a stand-in."

"A stand-in? What's that?" Ned asked.

"You know, the one who stands in for the star while they focus the lights and get the right camera exposures and stuff."

"Oh. Great. Is it more money?"

"I think so," I said, playing with my napkin. "A lot more work, though. I won't have that much time to hang, actually."

"Oh." Ned made a face. "That's too bad."

"Yes."

"Who are you standing in for?"

"Fiona Gibson."

"Oh!" Ned exclaimed. "So . . . that means you'll be, let me see, spending hours and hours with Brett Harley, holding you in his arms?"

"Um, I guess so, yeah, now that you mention it."

"Great," he said sarcastically. "Seriously . . . should I be worried, Nan?"

"Ned! Don't be ridiculous!"

"Am I being ridiculous?"

"Totally!"

"So I shouldn't be mad at you?"

"Oh, Ned, please. I've already got Bess mad at me, because she thought *she* should have gotten the job. She's probably telling George right now what a bad friend I am."

"Well . . . were you?" He gave me a serious look. He wasn't accusing me. He just wanted to know what I thought.

"I *do* want to be in this movie," I told him truthfully, "but not at the expense of my friendship with Bess. I just don't know how to make it right with her and still be in the film."

"Why don't you ask the casting director to make a switch—make you an extra, and Bess the stand-in?"

"They won't do it. She's not the right height, and they already have enough extras."

"Well, you could at least ask," he said.

"You're right," I said. "I will ask. After all, what's

one more extra, and Bess could wear a red wig and five-inch heels, and be a perfect stand-in, right?"

"Right."

"I'm going to ask about it first thing tomorrow," I said, pounding the table with my fist. "I'm going to ask them to make Bess the stand-in, and me a plain old extra."

"Good deal. In fact, why not ask about it tonight?"

"Tonight?"

"The whole cast and production crew is arriving at the Hotel Metropole at nine o'clock, in caravan from the airport. Everybody in town's going to be there."

"And every paparazzo, too—including you," I said, grinning. "You know, I think I'll call Bess, and see if she wants to—oh. Never mind."

"Hey, Nan, if you give her a call and tell her what you're going to do tonight, she'll forgive you."

"Good idea," I said. "That's exactly what I'm going to do."

I called Bess as soon as I got home. "Before you hang up," I said, "I want you to know that I'm going to the Metropole tonight to ask Gordon MacIntyre to give you my stand-in job."

"Oh, Nan . . ."

I could tell she was crying. "I'm so sorry it went down like it did today, Bess. I didn't mean to hurt you."

"I know," she said. "I've been thinking about it ever since, asking myself what I would have done in your shoes. I don't blame you for taking the stand-in job. I mean, a chance to get close to Brett Harley? I would have taken it in a second! And I'm sorry I left you standing there. George thinks I was being stupid, and she's right."

"No, no, you're not stupid."

"Thanks. And you're not a bad friend."

"Yes, I am."

"No, you're not."

"Yes, I—well, let's hope it goes well tonight," I said. "Meanwhile, are you going to be there?"

"Are you kidding? I wouldn't miss it. George is driving."

"Again? Come on, Bess, I can drive the three of us."

"It's all set, Nan. Just be at my place at eight thirty."

She might have forgiven me for being a bad friend, but Bess was not about to forgive me for running that yield sign. I'd have to take some special driving safety course before she'd agree to ride again with me behind the wheel.

"Hey, Bess, do you still have any old *Hollywood Gazettes* lying around?"

"Tons. Why?"

"I want to do a little reading up. You know, in case I get to talk to any of the stars—or to Gordon MacIntyre—I'll know a little something about them."

"Sure. I'll see what I can round up. See you at eight thirty?"

"I'll be there."

5

Night of the Paparazzi

At eight forty-six, the three of us finally left Bess's house. "Sorry," George said. "The engine wouldn't turn over. I guess I flooded it. I had to wait ten minutes before I tried it again."

"When are you ever going to get rid of this heap?" Bess asked, shaking her head in annoyance. "Now we're going to be late."

The crowd ringing the front of the Metropole was even bigger than the one at the community center. Everybody and their uncle wanted to get a glimpse of the biggest stars in Hollywood. Police were everywhere. I spotted Chief McGinnis hanging out right by the entrance. He's hard to miss: 6'3", two hundred and fifty pounds or so, big shock of white hair, red cheeks and nose, and bushy dark eyebrows.

He didn't see me, which was just as well. We don't get along, and I knew he didn't want me anywhere near this movie.

Too bad. Here I was.

"Yikes!" George said. "Listen, I'm going to drop you two off here and go find a place to park. If I don't find you, look for me afterward in the parking lot over by the pier."

"You mean you're not even *coming*?" Bess said in disbelief.

"You know, I'll get over it if I don't get to see Brett," George said with a smirk. "I'm just not into all this Hollywood glitz."

"I just don't get you, George," Bess said disapprovingly. "What is *wrong* with you, anyway?" Bess and I hopped out of the car, and George took off.

I could see we were going to have a hard time getting to the front row of this enormous crowd. But I needn't have worried—nobody can stop Bess. When she's determined to get somewhere, look out world!

"If I get Brett Harley's autograph, I'll just die!" she said, grabbing my hand and pulling me forward.

There had to be a thousand people there, but Bess was all elbows and saying "Excuse me," and pretty soon, we were standing right behind the ropes with the paparazzi and the police. Chief McGinnis noticed me, and I saw him flinch with annoyance and surprise before covering it up and giving me a polite smile and a little nod.

Too bad for you, Chief, I thought. I'm in the movie—as a *professional.* You can't keep me away, much as you'd like to.

There were a couple of TV crews doing interviews with the crowd, as well as reporters with microphones and notepads, making the best out of a long wait. Way at the other end of the mob, I saw Ned, taking pictures of River Heights citizens who'd shown up for the big arrival. I waved, but he didn't see me.

Suddenly Dierdre Shannon popped up beside us. "Hello, Nancy," she greeted me, her tone dripping with poison. "Hello, Bess. Still hoping to get discovered? Too bad you couldn't do it the legit way, like me and Nancy."

"Leave Nancy out of this," Bess said, forgiving me like the good friend she was. "And you know I'm way more talented than you are. Who got the lead in *Grease* last year, huh?"

"Shut up," Dierdre snapped as Bess smiled, victorious this time.

At about 9:15, two vans pulled up, followed by a couple of chartered buses. Several men and women began to step out, lugging their suitcases. "Who are they?" Bess wondered. "Are they famous? Do I need their autographs?"

"They're the production crew, duh," said Dierdre. "If they were famous, would they be riding in buses and vans? Wouldn't all these photographers be taking pictures?"

"Oh. I guess you're right. But if they're the crew, where's all their equipment?" asked Bess.

"You mean like cameras and stuff? What are you, mental? They don't bring it to the hotel." Now it was Dierdre's turn to flash a triumphant smile.

After the buses and vans pulled away, the limos started coming. The first held Sylvia Trout, along with three character actors I recognized from small parts in other movies. The cameras started popping. Even though these actors weren't big names, they were recognizable faces, and that was apparently good enough.

"Omigosh!" Bess gasped. "I saw her once on *Desperate Daughters*! She got strangled and dumped in a clothes dryer!" She jumped up and down, waving her autograph book, which she'd been holding ever since we got out of the car. "Yoo-hoo! Whatever your name is—over here!"

Of course, hundreds of other people were also yelling and waving their books—and we hadn't even reached the climax of the evening yet.

Then a big stretch limo rolled up, and Tina emerged, followed by Gordon MacIntyre. The whole crowd roared, yelling, "Gordon! I love you, Gordon!" I started getting shoved every which way. The director waved to the crowd, loving every minute.

I'd meant to approach him, to ask whether he'd give Bess my stand-in job and make me an extra instead, but I could see that there was no way I could get near him now. I'd have to wait for tomorrow to find a moment on the set to talk to him then.

Gordon put his arm around Tina, who beamed a huge smile for the photographers, as if she were his girlfriend. I wondered if she really was. She looked a bit frazzled, come to think of it. I wondered if she and Gordon had been making out in the back of the limo. . . . There wasn't much time to get a better look, though, because within seconds, the two of them had disappeared inside the hotel.

The crowd moaned, disappointed, but not for long. Another huge stretch limo pulled up, and out popped the truly gorgeous Fiona Gibson. Immediately the crowd shifted its focus. The flashbulbs blinded me (and everyone else, I'm sure). Fiona, red-headed and looking even prettier in person than in her films, blew kisses to everyone before slowly making her way up the line on the left, signing autographs and shaking hands.

Bess had joined the crush of people closing in

around Fiona. I have to say, they really did look alike, aside from the height and hair color. I saw Fiona catch sight of Bess and say something—probably just that. Bess glowed like she'd been lit up from the inside with a thousand-watt bulb. She turned to me, waving her signed autograph book, and I gave her a big thumbs-up.

The crowd was about three-quarters female, and mostly under thirty. I say this to explain what happened next. Another limo pulled up to the curb, and this time, out came Brett Harley. What happened next was truly amazing.

The noise was deafening, first of all. But then the crowd surged forward, turning into an instant mob. The police tried to keep them back, but it was no use. I looked around for Bess, but couldn't see her anymore. I only hoped she was all right.

The crowd's surge had left me at the rear. There was about twenty feet between me and the swaying mass of humanity that surrounded Brett Harley. And that was fine with me—let Bess get bumped and bruised for an autograph. I'd go back to the parking lot and find George.

I turned around, and was suddenly blinded by a camera flash.

"Hel-lo there!" came an oily, cheery voice.

"Geez!" I said, my hands covering my throbbing eyes. "Couldn't you have warned me?"

"Sorry," the voice said, "but the best shots always come when the subject is surprised."

"Huh? What are you talking about? Do I look like Fiona Gibson or something?"

"Not really. But you're going to be her stand-in, aren't you?"

"Hey! How did you find that out?" I asked, my vision beginning to clear. I could sort of make him out now. He was short, fat, bald, at least fifty years old, and sweating like a pig. His teeth were brown and stained, and didn't look too clean either. He held an old-fashioned flash camera in one hand and a microphone in the other. Around his neck hung an old portable tape recorder.

"I'm in with Sylvia Trout," he explained. "She pointed you out to me. It'll be a nice little angle on my story—*exclusive*."

"Right," I said. "And you are?"

"Oh, pardon me," he said, fishing a grease-stained business card out of his pocket and giving it to me.

"I can't read it," I said. "I'm still half-blind."

"Sorry about that, but like I said . . . Anyway, I'm Sidney Green. Call me Sid." He held out a hand for me to shake. It was as sweaty as his face.

Yuck. A real paparazzo had found me—and this one looked to be the lowest of the low.

"Who do you work for, Sidney?" I asked, ignoring his instructions to call him Sid as if we were best friends.

"*Hollywood Gazette,*" he said.

Well. That was impressive.

"Oh, yeah, I'm in with all the biggies. Brett, Fiona—we're all on a first name basis. Gordie and I, we're like that!" He crossed his fingers to illustrate his point.

My eyes had recovered by now, and I checked out his card. "How come it says 'freelance photographer/reporter'? Shouldn't it say '*Hollywood Gazette*'?"

"Oh . . . well . . . I'm branching out lately," he said.

Something about his tone told me he was lying. I wondered if they'd fired him or something. . . . *I* would have. I mean, he clearly hadn't washed in some time, or brushed his teeth, either. Not exactly a good representative for a popular (if trashy) magazine. I was just starting to feel sorry for him when he opened his mouth again.

"And what's your name, little lady?"

"First of all, I'm not a 'little lady,' okay? This is the twenty-first century, in case you didn't notice."

"A little old-world politeness never hurt," he said, offended.

"This isn't the Old World, and I wouldn't call shooting off a flash in my face without warning polite."

He was undeterred. "And your name is?"

I sighed, giving up, knowing he'd never let me alone until I told him. "Nancy Drew."

"Nancy Drew," he repeated into his mic. "Pleasure to meet you. I wonder if you'd agree to do a running interview—you know, a fresh angle on the film shoot, day by day."

I was about to give him the total brush-off, when I reconsidered. "I'll tell you what," I said. "I'll share inside information with you, if you'll do the same for me. You know, tell me everything you know about Brett and Fiona and 'Gordie.'"

"Sure thing!" he said, giving me his best rotten-toothed smile. His breath nearly knocked me over. I took two steps back, but he took two steps forward. There was no getting away from this guy. *Period.*

"You start," I said. "Tell me something I don't already know."

"Okay," he said, putting his mic in his pocket and shutting off his recorder. "How 'bout I tell you about Angelica?"

"Angelica? What about her?"

"Well, what do you already know?"

"I know she's a huge star, and she was Brett's girlfriend before Fiona."

"Correct!" he said with a nod of his head. "But did you know that she hasn't been seen for three weeks?"

"What?"

"Ah, so you *didn't* know!"

"Do they suspect foul play?"

"No, she left word she was going on vacation—but she didn't say where or when she'd be back."

"Hmm."

"Juicy, huh? Wanna know what I think?"

"What do you think?"

"I think she's jealous of Fiona. In fact, I know it for a fact. She was devastated by the breakup with Brett—totally destroyed. And then when he hooked up with Fiona, her archrival—"

"They're archrivals?"

"You really don't know much about what's going on, do you."

"Not really. Not in Hollywood, anyway."

"It shows. Anyway, as I was about to tell you, Angelica was so jealous after Brett hooked up with Fiona that she started *stalking* them."

"Stalking them? Are you sure?" I know I hadn't heard anything about that from Bess, who had told me everything else there was to know about Brett and Fiona and Angelica.

"I almost got a shot of her staring through the hedge to Brett's house, you know, while Brett and Fiona were inside. But Angelica saw me just in time and ducked away before I could snap it." He sighed, disappointed. "I tried to get the magazine to print the story, but they wouldn't—not without the photo to prove it."

Funny, I thought. Those celebrity rags were always printing stuff with no proof whatsoever and getting sued over it half the time.

The more time I spent with Sidney, the more I mistrusted him. Something about him wasn't quite right. I just couldn't put my finger on what it was. . . .

He wasn't finished, either. "Did you know Angelica was originally supposed to be the lead in this picture—you know, opposite Brett. But when he broke up with her, Angelica quit."

"And Fiona stepped right in?"

"That's how they got together—just three months ago, at the very start of filming. Gordon MacIntyre brought her in. Which is odd, because Fiona had dumped *him* for Brett a while back."

"Whoa. My head is spinning," I said—which it was. I could barely keep track of all the comings and goings!

"Anyway, if Angelica disappeared because she was

jealous, she shouldn't have bothered. Brett and Fiona are already fighting like cats and dogs. If you ask me, it's fifty-fifty odds their relationship crashes and burns before the movie wraps. Personally I think Gordie's just trying to keep them together long enough to finish filming the picture. That would be"—He checked his watch—"end of this week."

"So they're fighting, huh? But they've only been together—"

"Three months, that's right. Hey, at least you know *something*." He hoisted his camera strap over his shoulder and offered me his hand again.

Against my better instincts and my sense of hygiene, I shook it. After all, Sidney and I had just made a deal. Of course, I was only going to give him safe stuff—nothing that would ruin anyone's reputation. But I expected him to be a regular library of information for me. Information that was the real dirt—like who was out to kill this picture, and why?

"Well, I've told you enough for one night," he said. "Now you owe me. I want a full report tomorrow night, same time, same place—all about what it's like to work with Gordon, Fiona, and Brett. You know, little girl from little hick town rubs elbows with the big stars. . . ."

"I'm not a little girl, thank you. And River Heights isn't a hick town."

He snorted, the big-city know-it-all. I was really starting to hate paparazzi.

"So how did it go?" George asked me when I got back to the car.

"Fine."

"Did you see anybody?"

I filled her in on my evening, and just as I finished telling her about Sidney, Bess ran up to the car, out of breath with sheer excitement.

"I got her autograph!" she shrieked, deafening both me and George. "See? It says 'Fiona Gibson'!"

I gazed down at the scribbled signature. It could have been anybody's, to be perfectly honest, but Bess obviously didn't care about the penmanship.

"Why didn't you come?" Bess said. "It was so awesome! You missed everything!"

"No I didn't," George said, giving us both a mysterious smile.

"Huh? What do you mean?" Bess asked.

"I was parking the car when I nearly ran into this other guy's SUV. Turns out he's part of the film crew. His name's Sebastian Wright—he's kind of cute, actually, with a beard and long hair and stuff . . ."

"George!" Bess gasped.

"Anyway, we got to talking, and he's looking at my car, and he says, 'You know, that car is vintage.

It could be in the movie, because it's set in the seventies.' So I say, 'You mean, they'd pay me for using it?' And he says, 'Even better—they'll pay you as an extra to drive it, plus money for the car.' Apparently there's this big car-chase scene being filmed later in the week. So then he takes me to the hotel, to meet this lady Sylvia—"

"Sylvia Trout," I said needlessly.

"Yeah, that's her—and on the spot, she hands me a release to sign, and presto—I'm in the picture!"

"That's fantastic, Geo—"

I stopped in midsentence, seeing the look in Bess's eyes.

"Wait," she said, "let me get this straight—*you're* in the movie, making *extra* money for your disgusting old car; Dierdre Shannon, my favorite person in the world is in it, too; Nancy here is *Fiona's stand-in*; and I'm out on the street with nothing but a stupid autograph?"

"Wait, I didn't tell you the rest," George said sheepishly.

"You mean there's *more*?" Bess moaned.

"Um, yeah. See, it turns out Sebastian is the pyrotechnic guy on the movie—the one who sets up and sets off all the explosions, handles the guns and knives and stuff. He said at the end of the week, they're blowing up a whole building downtown for the grand finale!"

"Wow," I said, suddenly all ears. If someone was trying to sabotage the movie, or hurt people associated with it, what better way? Clearly Sebastian was an important person for me to meet—and to keep an eye on, maybe through George . . .

"He said he'd give me a tour of the set and show me all his pyro stuff—*if* I went out with him tomorrow night."

"And you said yes?" Bess asked, alarmed.

George blushed and shrugged. "Like I said, he's kind of cute," she admitted.

"George! You don't know this guy from Adam!" Bess said. "How do you know he's not an ax murderer or something?"

"Oh, come on, Bess," George said. "He seems like a nice guy—although there was something vaguely mysterious about him. . . ."

"See?" Bess said. "You're proving my point!"

"Do you think he could show us too?" I asked, ignoring Bess's hysterics.

"I'm pretty sure he would," George said, grinning.

"There you go, Bess," I said. "Cheer up. You're going to get a guided tour of the set."

"Great," Bess said miserably. "Hey, Nan, you didn't talk to Gordon MacIntyre about me, like you said you were going to."

"Um, no," I confessed. "You saw how quickly he disappeared into the hotel—I couldn't get to him. But tomorrow I will, first chance I get."

"You promise?"

"I promise."

Bess sighed, resigned to her fate. "If I don't get into this movie, I'll just die."

And if *I* didn't do my job on this movie—my *real* job—someone else might very well die.

6

New Friends, New Enemies

I drove myself to the community center the next morning. George's scene with her car wasn't until later in the week, and Bess . . . well, she wasn't even *in* the movie yet—and unless I could convince Gordon MacIntyre otherwise, she was never going to be.

I parked, found the bus and Sylvia Trout, and checked in.

"Nancy Drew . . ." She checked the list on her clipboard. "Oh, you're the stand-in for Fiona. . . . They need you in Costume. You'd better go find the trailer. It's back on the street over there. You'll see it—it's got a sign."

I grabbed a coffee and doughnut—they were laid out on a table next to the bus—and headed up Bluff Street, passing several trailers along the way. All of them had their engines running. There was no other way to keep the air-conditioning going, and today was going to be a scorcher. You could tell, even though the sun was barely up.

A sign on the first trailer read BRETT HARLEY. The next one read FIONA GIBSON. I wondered if they were inside. I have to admit, it was kind of thrilling to know that in just a few hours, I'd be on a first-name basis with them both. Wow, was I lucky!

Then I thought of Bess. The third trailer's sign read GORDON MACINTYRE, DIRECTOR. I knocked, and the door opened, but it wasn't him. It was his assistant director, Tina.

"What?" she asked, impatient.

"Is Mr. MacIntyre here? I, um, need to see him about something."

"He's busy. You can see me about it." She folded her arms and stood blocking the door.

"Um, sorry, but it's . . . I just need to speak with him."

"Uh-huh. Well, he's kind of busy, y'know? We're shooting a film here. Speaking of which . . ."

"Oh, I know. I'm in the film. Remember me? I'm Fiona's stand-in."

"Oh. Well in that case, get yourself over to Costume. We need you on the set in half an hour."

I knew that even if Gordon MacIntyre was in that

trailer, she wasn't going to let me near him. I would have to wait a little longer for my chance to speak with him.

I continued on to the next trailer, which had a sign reading COSTUMES. The door was open, and inside, I could hear Fiona's familiar voice, talking a mile a minute.

"I think he's just so brave, don't you? I mean, if *I* got an e-mail like that, I would just totally lose it! I told him, 'Sweetie, you know it's that witch Angelica, don't you? She just can't stand it that we're in love.' And you know what he says to me? 'It's not her.' Can you believe that? He still has a thing for her!"

"Oh, honey, I don't think so," another woman's deep voice replied. "He's nuts about you. You can just see it when you're together."

"You think so?" Fiona sounded pleased, but not entirely sure. "I wonder . . ."

I knocked on the open door. "Come in," the woman with the deep voice said.

Going up the three stairs, I entered the trailer, which was so crammed with costumes that you could barely take a step in any direction. About halfway down the aisle (if you could call it that) stood Fiona Gibson herself, wearing an outfit straight out of the seventies—right down to the bell-bottom pants, complete with braiding.

The other woman, obviously the costume mistress, had a mouth full of pins, and was trying to make the costume fit perfectly on Fiona. She was fussing with every nook and cranny of the blouse, and Fiona had to keep moving her arms around to avoid getting pricked.

"Hi," I said. "I'm Nancy Drew, your stand-in?"

"Oh, hi!" Fiona said, giving me a million-watt smile and a little wave. "Nice to meet you, Nancy!"

"While I finish Fiona off," the costume mistress said, "why don't you grab that outfit off the rack and try it on." She nodded her head toward an outfit identical to the one Fiona was wearing.

I followed her orders, and soon, Fiona and I looked like a pair of almost-identical twins.

"Will you get a load of the two of us?" she said, giggling and pointing at the full-length mirror. "Aren't we a pair?" I had to admit, it was a little weird.

"How's yours fit?" the costume lady asked me.

"Fine," I said.

"'Cause it doesn't have to be perfect," she explained. "Just a reasonable resemblance."

"Oh, most definitely!" Fiona said, giggling again and nudging me like we were already best friends.

I thought guiltily of Bess. It should have been *her* standing here with Fiona, not me. This wasn't my dream, it was hers.

Still, there was my investigation of the threatening e-mails to consider. I'd just learned something I would never have heard if I hadn't been Fiona's stand-in—namely, that Brett didn't think it was Angelica who'd written them, even though she was the one with the most obvious motive.

A walkie-talkie blasted out static. Then: "Costume?"

The costume lady grabbed the walkie-talkie and said, "Costume here."

"Stand-in ready?"

"Ready."

"Okay, she's needed on the set in five."

"Copy that." She looked over at me. "Hear that?"

"Uh-huh. Where's the set?"

"Down past the bus, across the street and around the corner, by the drugstore."

"Mason's?"

"That's the one. Better get down there pronto."

"I'll walk you as far as my trailer," Fiona offered.

As soon as we were back on the street, she slipped an arm through mine. "So," she said, "this is such a cute town! You must totally *love* living here."

"Yeah, it's . . . great," I said, a little thrown off by how unbelievably friendly she was being.

"I wish *I* could live a normal life," she confided. "It's such a huge pain being a star."

"It must be hard to find privacy," I sympathized.

"Totally."

"What with all the paparazzi . . ."

"Oh, they're just impossible! I wish they'd just treat me and Brett like normal, everyday people."

No you don't, I thought, remembering how she'd acted at the Metropole the night before. Not really. You love the attention.

"Well, I'll see you later," she said as she reached for the door of her trailer. "Keep my seat warm." She opened the door, then suddenly stepped back and let out a little shriek.

There was Brett Harley, his hand out like he'd been reaching for the door from inside just as she opened it. "Whoa! Um, hi there!" he said, his face going red.

"Brett, sweetie, what are you doing here?" Fiona asked. "Aren't you supposed to be on set?"

"They can wait," he said, taking her in his arms and bending her over backward.

"Not now, snookums!" she said, slapping at him playfully. "I'm in full makeup—you'll smudge it!"

He pulled her back upright, then stopped, seeing me for the first time. "Whoa—either I'm seeing double or you must be Fiona's stand-in."

"That's me," I said, nodding.

Then, to my surprise, and certainly Fiona's, he let

go of her, so suddenly that she almost fell over. He came over and took my hand in his, and said, "I'm Brett. What's your name, cutie pie?"

"Um, Nancy," I said. "Nancy Drew."

"Excellent," he said, flashing me his famous smile. "I look forward to working with you, Nancy. See you on the set, and tell Gordo I'm on my way."

"Sure thing," I said, backing away. As I did, I caught Fiona shooting daggers at me. I guessed we weren't going to be best friends after all, thanks to Brett and his flirty ways.

Well, it was too late to do anything about it. Anyway, now she'd be glad when Bess showed up tomorrow to do the job instead of me.

I turned and started walking down the hill, but I could still hear their voices behind me—mostly Fiona's.

"What did you think you were doing?" she demanded.

"Baby, take it easy—" Brett began.

"Don't call me 'baby'!" she cut him off. "You think you can flirt with every cute girl you meet? What about us?"

"Come on, babe, don't get hysterical. . . ."

"I am not hysterical!" she yelled hysterically. "And what were you doing in my trailer?"

"Just looking for you," he replied.

I wondered if she believed him. I sure didn't. Fiona and I had been standing in front of that trailer for at least two minutes before the door was opened. It only would have taken him two seconds to see she wasn't there, and leave.

"You are such a liar!" Fiona screamed. "You lied to Angelica too. That's why she went crazy and started stalking us—it's all your fault!"

"She wasn't stalking us, babe," Brett said. "She was just upset—"

"And what about those threatening e-mails?" Fiona went on. "You *know* she wrote them. It's her revenge on Gordon for giving me the part, and on you for going out with me."

"Babe, even if she did write them, she'd never do anything for real—I know Angelica. She's a sweetheart."

"*Sweetheart?*"

"Babe, wait—I—"

I heard the door of Fiona's trailer slam, and then Brett banging on it. I wanted to linger there to see if I could pick up any more information, but I was late, and the last thing I wanted was to get fired.

Continuing on my way, I reached the bus, where the extras—maybe thirty of them—were all surrounding the coffee and food tables like a bunch of hungry vultures. I kept going, avoiding that mob scene.

In front of Mason's Drugstore, I found Gordon MacIntyre, Tina, and a couple dozen cameramen, gaffers, lighting techies, and assorted production assistants. Halfway down the block, a cordon of River Heights police kept the local gawkers away from the set.

"Here's the stand-in for Fiona," Tina yelled when she saw me. "Over here, Nora."

"Um, it's Nancy," I said. "Nancy Drew."

"Whatever. Over here, in the light. That's it—facing Brett."

I looked. Brett was still back at the trailer, fighting with Fiona. I didn't see anyone who looked like his stand-in, either. But there was an *X* made out of tape on the ground where I guessed he was supposed to be standing.

"Face the wall," Tina said.

I got into position, and stood stock-still while the technicians adjusted their lights and camera lenses. After a minute or so, Gordon MacIntyre walked up to me. "You all right, young lady? You need some coffee or something? I can send someone to get it."

I had to smile. He was so considerate. "That'd be great," I said. "But Mr. MacIntyre?"

"Yes?"

"There's something else I need to ask you."

"Well, hurry it up, then. We've got to get going here. Time is money."

"I know that—I'll try to keep this short. You see, my friend Bess Marvin loves your movies like crazy, but she didn't get picked to be an extra. She's a dead ringer for Fiona, and I was wondering if, maybe, I could be just an extra, and *she* could be Fiona's stand-in instead."

There. I'd asked him. I could feel the blood pounding in my temples and my cheeks blushing red. He stared at me for a long moment, and then a sweet, tender smile crossed his lips, and his jewel-like eyes bored right through me.

"What did you say was your name?" he asked.

"Nancy," I said with a shaky voice. "Nancy Drew."

"I'll tell you what, Nancy Drew. If you do something for me, I'll do something for you."

Yes! Bess was going to be so happy!

"Okay, I guess. What?"

"I'll make sure your friend Betsy gets hired, okay? As an extra, though—*not* as a stand-in."

"It's *Bess*, not Betsy. But—"

"No buts. That's my final offer."

Oh, well. I guessed it was better than nothing. Bess would definitely be pleased, if not overjoyed.

"That'd be great, Mr. MacIntyre."

"Call me Gordon, Nancy. Please." He gave me that look again.

"Well, thank you . . . Gordon." I could barely get the words out; he was so handsome.

"I'll do it, *if* you'll let me take you to dinner tonight after the shoot."

"If I . . . *what?*"

I couldn't believe it. He'd just asked me out! Gordon MacIntyre! Sure, he was at least fifteen years older than me, but—but *Gordon MacIntyre*!

Wait, wait a minute—I already had a boyfriend. A great one—Ned Nickerson. I couldn't just go out with someone else!

Or could I? After all, Bess would be destroyed if she didn't at least get to be an extra. Especially since Dierdre and George got to, and I got to be Fiona's stand-in.

Besides, I was really here to investigate those threatening e-mails, one of which had been sent to Gordon MacIntyre. How was I supposed to get any information if I turned down opportunities like this one?

Convincing myself that I was doing it for Bess and that it was all strictly business on my part, I said, "Okay—but don't you think Bess could be the stand-in, and me be the extra?"

He laughed softly and shook his head. "Not a

chance," he said, mesmerizing me with his eyes. "I've got the girl I want, and it's you, Nancy Drew."

Well, you can just imagine the effect those words had on me, Ned or no Ned. I quickly got it together, but not quickly enough to escape the penetrating gaze of Tina, who clearly was not happy with me.

Oh, well, I thought. I've just made one friend and one enemy, so it comes out even.

Not quite, of course. Gordon seemed interested in me, but that didn't make him a friend. As far as I was concerned, he was just a subject of my investigation—someone who might need my protection.

On the plus side, I'd gotten Bess the job as an extra. As long as she didn't find out about my "date" with Gordon MacIntyre, she was sure to feel better about me as a friend.

"Where's Brett's stand-in?" Tina shouted at Sylvia Trout, who was standing right next to her.

Sylvia was so startled, her gigantic silver wig drooped to one side, and she had to correct it. "He seems to be, er, late."

"Well, get someone else, pronto!"

"Tina, calm down," Gordon said, putting a hand on her shoulder.

She yanked herself away. "I'm perfectly calm," she

said with an icy voice, and shot me another poisonous glance.

"Hey, all!" It was Brett. He seemed bright and cheerful in contrast to the rest of us. "No need for a stand-in—here's the real thing, in person!" Turning to me, he winked, flashed his sexiest smile, and said, "Hello, gorgeous. Ready to get to work?"

With Gordon shaping the scene, Brett took me in his arms, and we struck a pose, with him dipping me, my head dangling backward, him leaning over me.

Up close, I could see that while Brett was still smiling, his eyes were not joining in. They held something else—something darker. Was it anger? Fear? I couldn't tell, but I suspected his good cheer was as phony as a three-dollar bill.

That red area on his cheek, in the shape of a hand? Something told me he and Fiona had had a rip-roaring fight after I left her trailer.

"Now kiss her," Gordon ordered as he peered through the camera lens.

"Ready?" Brett asked.

"Huh? Wait a min—"

Too late. He planted his lips on mine, and there was no escape. Figuring I might as well enjoy an opportunity millions of girls would have given their eye teeth for, I sort of kissed him back.

"Okay, back to one! Let's do it once more, with the lights a bit lower."

Gordon's voice reached me through a velvety haze. Brett let me loose, and I stood up straight and breathed deeply, trying not to pass out.

Oh my. It suddenly hit me. In the space of ten minutes, I'd just been asked out by Gordon MacIntyre and kissed by Brett Harley!

Looking around, I saw that a small crowd of people had gathered about three stores up the block, on the other side of the rope. To one side of them were a bunch of paparazzi.

And there, in the middle of them, his camera hanging limply from his neck, his face a mask of pain and betrayal, stood my wonderful boyfriend, Ned Nickerson.

"Ned!" I yelled. I wanted to go to him, to explain what had just happened. But I never got the chance.

"Let's do it once more for lighting. Nancy!" Tina snapped, and once again I felt Brett's strong arms around me.

As I was dipped backward, the last thing I saw before Brett's lips locked onto mine was Ned turning his back to me and walking away.

7

The Volcano Erupts

I *couldn't* go after him. I mean, kiss or no kiss, I was working, right? Finally, after about six or seven times, Fiona showed up to do the actual kissing scene.

I could see she was still mad at Brett. On the first take, she barely gave the kiss an effort.

"Cut! Cut! Come on, Fiona!" Gordon complained. "That's the lamest kiss I've ever seen. It was hotter with the stand-in, for goodness' sake!"

Oops. That was the wrong thing to say. Fiona glared at me so hard I thought I would spontaneously combust.

"You're an actress, darling," Gordon said—with a touch of sarcasm, it seemed to me. "Let's see that supposed talent you're so famous for."

As if to show him, Fiona then laid an amazing lip-lock on Brett, which went on and on . . . and on . . . It was as if they hadn't quarreled at all. In the kissing department, at least, Fiona deserved an Oscar.

"Cut!" Gordon said. "Great, check the gate, please."

When Tina told him it looked good, he said, "Fantastic, that's a keeper. Nice work, Fiona." That touch of sarcasm again, and I noticed he didn't mention Brett.

"Back to the bus," Tina ordered me. "Lunch break's in twenty."

I have to admit I didn't go right back to the bus. I know that's unprofessional, but my real job here was not as a stand-in, after all. Besides, I needed to call Ned right away. I couldn't stand the thought of him hating me for kissing Brett Harley.

I walked down the alleyway to the right of Mason's. There was a trailer there with a table in front of it that held different kinds of electronic timers and explosive charges. In front of the table stood a tall, thin bearded guy in his twenties.

"Sebastian?" I guessed. "Sebastian Wright?"

"That's me," he said cheerfully. "And you are?"

"Nancy Drew. George Fayne's friend."

"George with the car?" he asked. "Yeah, she talked about you. Hi, nice to meet you."

"You were going to give her a tour of the set, she said."

"Uh-huh."

"And . . . what's all this, speaking of tours?"

"This? Oh, I'm laying out the stuff for this afternoon's pyrotechnics."

"What's happening this afternoon?"

"Um, there's a shot of Fiona almost getting blown up when her car explodes outside the restaurant."

"*Really?*" I was *so* glad I'd stopped by. "Tell me, how do you make sure nobody gets hurt?"

He laughed. "Oh, well, that would take a while to explain. But basically they're just blank charges for the most part, thrown in with some flaming flash stuff and some fake auto glass made out of glycerine there . . ."—He pointed out a front and back windshield.—"And the stuntpeople know what they're doing, so hopefully nobody gets hurt."

"Oh, so Fiona's not really going to be in any danger?"

"Nah. Brett's the one who always does his own stunts. He came up as a stuntman, actually. But Fiona's notorious for being a bit of a diva. She hasn't done any of her own stunts for years."

"I see."

"Of course, she *is* going to have to be part of the burning warehouse scene on Friday. Gordon told her to just 'suck it up and be a man.' Ha! That was hilarious. 'Be a man.' Fiona Gibson. I like that. . . ."

"Hey, Sebastian?"

"Yeah?"

"Is there some problem around this shoot that you know of? Because everyone seems kind of spooked—talking about threats and stuff . . ." I was trying to be general to draw him out without him suspecting my intentions.

"I wouldn't know," he said. "I'm new here. Gordon always worked with this one pyro guy, but after that horrendous accident on his last film, he swore he'd never work with him again. So, here I am."

"What actually happened?"

"I forget, it was so long ago. Something about a leftover charge going off and severing the dead girl's cable."

"Cable?"

"Yeah, it was on this cliff. They'd staged a landslide earlier that day, with charges in the cliff going off to make it look natural. Then that night, they were shooting the stunt girl rappeling down the cliff, and the charge went off. Something like that."

"Thanks, Sebastian," I said. "I'd like to join you and George for that little tour, if you don't mind."

"Fine with me if she's okay with it," he said, and waved to me as I continued down the alley.

Finding a private spot, I dialed Ned's cell number. His voice mail picked up.

"Ned, it's Nancy. What happened this morning . . . it wasn't a real kiss, Ned. He just . . . I didn't know he was going to—oh, never mind. Just, please, don't be upset, because it's *you* I care about, not anyone else—especially not Brett Harley. Okay, call me, okay? Bye."

Ugh, I sounded like such a geek. I was really disgusted with myself. I could only hope Ned would forgive me for allowing it to happen.

Next, I called Bess. She picked up on the first ring. Obviously she'd been waiting right by the phone for my call.

"Nancy!" she said breathlessly. "How did it go? What did he say?"

"Well," I said, "you're in the movie."

"AAAAHHHH! Yessss! Yes, yes, yes, yes, yes! I love you, Nan. You're the bestest friend in the whole wide—"

"Bess, wait—there's more."

"Huh?"

"I'm still Fiona's stand-in."

"But—"

"You're an extra. I'm sorry, but that's all I could get him to do."

"Oh." There was a long silence, and I knew what

she was thinking—that I could have just refused to be the stand-in. "Oh, okay . . . I guess. Thanks."

"He said he'd only do it if I stayed the stand-in. Really, it's the truth."

"Uh-huh. Well, okay." She sniffed back her tears, then giggled. "Just promise me you'll get me Brett's autograph, okay?"

"Totally!" I was so relieved, I could have melted into butter. Together with George, Bess really was one of my best friends in the whole world. To lose her would have been a disaster—especially the way things were going with Ned.

"So when do I have to show up?" she asked.

"I don't know," I said. "We're shooting right now, and there's this big car-chase scene they're shooting later in the week. You'd better just get down here and speak to Tina or Sylvia."

"I'm on my way. Oh, Nan, you forgot to take those old *Hollywood Gazettes* with you. Girl, you are so absent-minded it's pathetic."

We shared a laugh. "I know, I know," I said. "I'm lost without you, Bess—bring them along with you. See you soon."

"Say, Nan, what are you doing tonight? I thought we could all hang out in the lobby of the Metropole and do a little stargazing."

"Um, I can't tonight. I'm busy."

"Busy? With what?"

I *couldn't* tell her the truth—no way would she have understood. And I wasn't ready to tell her about my investigation yet, either. Sometimes it's better to keep your secrets until the right moment. And this was definitely one of those times.

The afternoon shoot featured me standing in—with Fiona doing the actual take—exiting Olde River Jewelers and opening the door of a black convertible. We finished shooting the scene pretty quickly, and then Fiona disappeared into her trailer.

I hung around for a while, eager to see what was going to happen next. A stunt double was going to repeat Fiona's actions, except that this time, when she opened the door, the car would "explode" into flames.

Gordon MacIntyre went over to inspect the car, to make sure it was ready for the stuntwoman's entrance. Then suddenly, without any warning, there was a huge flash and a loud *boom*!

8

Dinner for Two

Gordon flew backward and slammed against the brick wall of the jewelry store. Everyone screamed, and Tina rushed to his side.

Slowly, he got to his feet and began inspecting himself. "I'm fine . . . I think," he said, dusting off his tattered clothes and checking to see if he still had any eyelashes.

"Fine? Are you *berserk*? You could have been burned to a crisp!" Tina said semihysterically. "Where's that pyro guy? Tell him he's fired!"

"No, no, no," Gordon soothed her. "It's okay, Tina. No harm done. Let's not make a federal case out of it."

"Gee, I don't know what happened!" Sebastian said,

bending over the car to check the charges he'd planted there. "One of these must have been defective. . . ."

I wondered. Someone had sent a threatening e-mail to Gordon, after all. Maybe they'd gone the next step and just missed killing him.

I added Sebastian Wright to my list of suspects, and determined I needed to ask Gordon some probing questions at dinner tonight.

A police squad, led by Chief McGinnis himself, came running out of the police station just up the block, while the fire detail that had been stationed nearby all day inspected the damaged vehicle. The swarm of paparazzi struggled to get close enough for pictures while the crew's production assistants struggled to keep them at bay.

"It's all right, I tell you," Gordon insisted to Chief McGinnis. "No harm done. It was just a charge that prematurely went off. No need to be concerned. Let's bring in another vehicle and start over."

Finally, the police and fire detail left, along with the paparazzi, and things settled down. Another vehicle was brought in, and Sebastian got to work, rigging it with fresh charges.

Just then, Fiona burst back onto the set, waving a piece of paper. "I'm sick and tired of this, Gordon!" she screamed, tears rolling down her face. "I can't take the stress. You can finish this stupid film without me because I quit!"

"What are you talking about, Fiona?" Gordon said. "You can't quit—we're two days away from wrapping! What in the world's got you so upset, anyway?"

"This!" she said, thrusting the piece of paper at him. I was close enough to see that it was a sheet of fancy stationery. "Go on, read it. Tell them all what it says!"

He read the note, but remained silent, so Fiona filled us all in herself. "It says, 'You're gonna die out there. Quit now if you value your life.' Nice, huh?" She turned back to Gordon. "You gonna give that to the police? Because if you don't, I'm outta here *today*!"

Gordon managed to calm her down, promising to hand the note straight over to the police, and to ask for a heavy security presence for the rest of the shoot. That was fine by me. As long as I was free to operate on the inside, keeping the outside world away could only be good.

I was also glad the police would have something to analyze for fingerprints and handwriting. E-mails are much harder to track. By switching to paper, the would-be killer, who had now threatened the lives of three very famous people, had made their first mistake.

Before I left for the day, Gordon took down my address and told me he'd pick me up at my house at eight o'clock. I had three hours to get ready, so I figured I could spare two to go over some of Bess's old *Hollywood Gazettes*.

What did I learn? Well, I found out that Fiona Gibson actually *was* hysterical. She'd been hospitalized for nervous breakdowns twice; once as a teenager and once—get this—on Gordon MacIntyre's last movie. Apparently she had been the one scheduled to do the fatal stunt. The only reason she didn't die was because she chickened out at the last moment. No wonder she'd stopped doing her own stunts after that!

I also learned that Brett Harley had once been a member of a notorious street gang, and had even done time in state prison for assault and battery. I have to admit I was pretty shocked by that. Even though Brett seemed to have left his past behind, I now knew he had once been capable of violence.

Oh, and there was one other thing. The oldest magazines—dating five years back (Bess is such a packrat!)—had a series of articles by none other than Sidney Green. Most of them were about how Gordon MacIntyre's carelessness, recklessness, and disregard for other people's welfare had resulted in the death of this pretty young stuntwoman who had been killed on the set during an action shot.

Sidney's articles were vicious, slicing Gordon's character into tiny shreds. Either he was right about

Gordon (yikes!), or Sidney had some kind of personal grudge against him. I hoped it was the latter because otherwise I was about to go out to dinner with the worst human being in the entire world!

I showered and got dressed, and just as I was putting on my earrings, I heard a car horn downstairs. Looking out the window, I saw a white stretch limo, complete with sunroof, parked outside.

I did a last check in the mirror, wondering if Bess would give me her seal of approval. Then I headed downstairs and out the front door. No need to say good-bye to my dad—he still hadn't come home from work. I wondered if it had anything to do with the note that was sent to Fiona . . . .

A uniformed chauffeur got out and opened the door for me. Gordon was seated inside, looking changed and refreshed. "Hello, there," he said as I got in.

"Hi yourself," I said, accepting his kiss on the cheek, but sitting a safe distance away. "Where are we off to?"

"I thought we'd try the Mission Hill Inn. I hear they have terrific fusion cuisine."

"The Mission Hill Inn? Wow. I've only ever eaten there a couple times in my whole life—and I *live* here." It is by far the most expensive place for a hundred miles in any direction.

We rode up to the bluffs overlooking the Muskoka

River, where the restaurant was located, and got to our table by the picture windows just in time to take in the sunset. "Romantic, isn't it?" he said as we sat down.

"Uh-huh." I was getting more and more nervous by the minute. Pretty soon, I was going to have to tell him I had a boyfriend. But not yet—not until I'd gotten him to talk about . . . everything.

The waiter took our order (I let Gordon order for me—some French specialty he said was hard to get and shouldn't be missed) and left the two of us alone with only a candle between us.

He reached over and took both my hands in his. "Ah, it's wonderful to get away from all the stress of the shoot."

"Is it?"

"You have no idea, Nancy."

"What happened today, anyway?" I asked, pulling my hands away.

"You mean the explosion? Or Fiona's little hissy fit?"

"Um, both, I guess."

"Well, as to the explosion, this fellow Sebastian I took on just last week doesn't seem to know what he's—"

"Wait, wait—you say you only hired him last week?"

"Yes. My regular pyrotechic man . . . Well, he passed away in the middle of the shoot. Heart attack. Very sudden. So sad . . ."

"I'll say." Another death on a Gordon MacIntyre shoot. Either this guy was cursed, or someone was out to get him. I decided to find out which. "So the new guy . . . ?"

"He's local, supposedly. The studio sent him over as a replacement, so I don't suppose they can blame me for this one, although I'm sure they'd love to have an excuse."

"I . . . don't understand." I thought I did, but I wanted him to explain it.

"Are you a movie fan, Nancy?" he asked, taking my hand again and gazing at me as the sun's last rays glittered in his blue-green eyes. "Be honest—I won't be offended."

"Not a huge one," I admitted, letting go of his hand. I'm too busy fighting crime to spend many evenings in front of the tube or at the cineplex.

"I thought not. If you were, you would have heard about my . . . unfortunate history."

I gave him a quizzical look. "My last movie was five years ago," he said, sighing. "There was a terrible accident. A young girl died horribly, on my watch, due to a series of missteps and just plain bad luck. Of course, I felt responsible—in a general sense, that is. I'm the director, after all. I'm responsible for everything that happens on my set. On the other hand, the accident was caused by someone else's carelessness, not mine."

"Someone else's?"

"An explosive charge that should have been removed had remained in place, undetonated—and went off at the worst possible moment."

"Wait—you mean that same pyrotechnician who died last week was the one who—"

"Yes. I hired him for this movie, out of pity, really. You see, the . . . 'incident' ruined his career as well as mine. So once the studio gave me this chance, I felt I owed it to him . . . to give him a new lease on life as well."

"And now he's dead," I said.

"Yes. Awful, isn't it? It's like I'm cursed."

That word again . . .

"But, you see, no matter what obstacles there are, I've got to finish this film. It's my ticket back to the top, Nancy."

"Well, what about that letter Fiona got today?" I asked.

"Yes . . . it's a problem, I'll admit it. Someone seems determined to stop the shoot. But I'm not going to let them. Just a couple more days and we'll be home free. No more shooting, no more depending on stars with unstable personalities."

"Unstable? You mean Fiona?"

"I'm not giving away any secrets when I tell you she's been hospitalized twice for nervous breakdowns. No, I won't have to deal with her once we're done shooting. In fact, you did such a good job today that I have half a mind to fill in shots with you if she keeps up the diva routine."

"Oh, I'm sure that won't be necessary," I said. I was pretty sure I was blushing.

"Anyway, I can't wait till this week is over," he said. "After that, it'll be just me, in the editing room, putting it all together, safe from prying eyes . . . or saboteurs . . ."

"You think it was sabotage?" I asked him. "I mean, the mistimed flare that almost got you today?"

He shrugged. "It could have been an accident, but there's nothing accidental about those e-mails and that letter Fiona got." His expression grew dark, and I could see something hidden behind his gorgeous eyes . . . something like . . . *rage*. "Whoever it is, I won't let them steal my last, best chance in life."

He took my hand and grasped it tightly, gazing into my eyes. "I'm a man on a mission, Nancy, and nobody's going to stop me from finishing this picture."

I was held by his gaze, and couldn't look away no matter how hard I tried. Finally he took a deep breath and relaxed his hold. I slowly removed my hand and looked around, feeling guilty. Not that I expected to see Ned there, but I'd already been caught by him kissing Brett today. The last thing I needed was for him to somehow be here in the restaurant while Gordon MacIntyre held my hand and gazed deeply into my eyes.

Ned wasn't there, of course. Thank goodness for that. I did catch sight of Brett and Fiona, tucked away inside a private corner booth. They seemed to be arguing, although it was hard to tell. I wished we were sitting closer. I'd have loved to be a fly on the wall and overhear their conversation. But since I couldn't, I decided to concentrate on Gordon.

"Who do you think would try to sabotage the film?" I asked him.

"It's hard to say," he said, "but I have my enemies at the studio."

"They wouldn't destroy their own investment, would they?"

"Ah, but if they have to stop the shoot before it's finished, the insurance company would have to pay them back."

"I see . . . so once filming's over . . ."

"That's right. Once we're done here in River

Heights, nothing can stop this picture—or my return to the top." He took my hand again. "How'd you like to come out to Hollywood and visit me during editing?" he asked, leaning in toward me so that our faces were only a few inches apart.

This would have been the time to tell him I had a boyfriend, and that there was no way I was coming out to Hollywood to see him. But I never got the chance.

I heard a gasp from over my shoulder. Then, "I can't believe this—*Nancy*?"

That awful, piercing voice . . .

Knowing it was too late, I withdrew my hand from Gordon's and turned to face Dierdre Shannon, who was standing there with her father, the head of the country club, and her mother, the snobbiest socialite in River Heights.

"Hello, Mr. MacIntyre," Dierdre crooned, giving him her flirtiest smile.

"It's not what you think, Dierdre," I said.

"Oh, no?" she replied, smirking. "I'll bet it is. Even better, I'll bet Ned would think so too."

"Dierdre, you wouldn't—"

"Wouldn't I?" she said, the smirk turning itself into an evil grin. "You just watch me."

9

From Bad to Worse

After Gordon's chauffeur drove me straight back home (Gordon didn't argue—he had to be up at five A.M. for the next day's shoot), I tried Ned on his cell. No luck. Either he had it turned off, or he wasn't taking my calls.

This was a disaster of the first order. If Dierdre got to Ned before I did, he might break up with me before I even got a chance to explain. And I was ready to explain everything to him—including my investigation of the threats. Unlike Bess, Ned could keep a secret if I asked him to. But how could I explain if he wouldn't take my calls?

It was late, and there was that early call time tomorrow, so I was just about ready to turn in, but there was one more phone call I wanted to make first.

"Sidney? This is Nancy Drew. Remember me?"

"Hello, kitten. Got some good dish for me?"

"Uh, well, yes, actually." If I wanted to ask a favor of him—and I did—I had to do something for him first, and I knew it. That's the way people like Sidney work. "Fiona and Brett had a fight today."

"Oh, really! Do tell . . ."

Ugh. His tone was so sleazy it made me shiver with disgust.

"Some jealousy thing. That's all I know right now, but I'll try to get more."

"Well, it's a start," he said. "And now? Presumably, there's something you want from me, too, or you wouldn't have called. Am I right?"

"Yes," I admitted. "There is something. Um, if you happen to hear any rumors . . . romantic rumors, about me and Gordon MacIntyre . . ."

"You and Gordon MacIntyre?!"

"Or me and Brett Harley . . ."

"*Or* you and Brett?!"

"Just . . . don't print them, okay? Because I can tell you for sure, there's no truth to them—none whatsoever."

"Uh-huh . . . right. You know, Nancy, I've been around long enough to know that where there's smoke, there's usually fire."

"Well, not this time," I said.

"Nancy?"

"Yeah?"

"I can hear you blushing right through the phone line."

"Sidney—*please*?"

He sighed. "All right. But you owe me one, kid. A *big* one."

A few days later, George drove me and Bess to the set on Bluff Street, right near the Anvil Overlook. This was to be the day of the big car-chase scene, and that meant it was George's chance to be in the movie, complete with jalopy.

"I'm so excited!" she said as we drove, gazing at the panorama of the cliffs and the river on our right.

"I thought you didn't want to be in any trashy movies," Bess teased her.

"I still don't care about that part," George said. "It's just the money that I find exciting. New car, here I come!"

"You mean, new *used* car," Bess corrected her.

"Don't say 'used', say 'pre-owned'," George said. "It sounds much better that way."

"Different word, same car," Bess said. "Hey, here we are!"

Bess was excited too, since this was to be her first shot in the movie. Always optimistic, she had convinced herself that now that she was in the film, she was sure to be "discovered" and given a bigger role. I only hoped she wouldn't be too disappointed if it didn't happen.

Oh, sure, it had just happened to me the other day. But I was pretty sure lightning wasn't going to strike twice.

As for me, I had other worries on my mind. For one thing, there was Ned. And for another, there was the hidden saboteur. Either he or she was just trying to scare people, or they really meant business—in which case, today's car-chase scene would be a perfect time to strike.

"I went out with Sebastian last night," George announced.

"How was it?" I asked.

"Well, he asked me out again for tonight, so it couldn't have gone too badly."

"Wow, that's awesome!" Bess said. "Is he really cute?"

George smiled her signature half-smile. "He's not hideous."

"Be careful, George," I warned, thinking of the near-accident few days ago.

"Is he a good kisser?" Bess wondered.

"Shut up—I wouldn't know," George said, giving Bess a light punch in the arm.

"Ow!"

"He did tell me all about today's shot," she said. "Wanna hear, Nancy?"

"You know I do."

"Well, Brett's going to be driving this really hot Ferrari, chased by two other cars—they're the bad guys—and he does this super-tight spinning turn just at the bottom of Sutter Avenue, right in front of the overlook, and the two pursuing cars miss it, then slam into that brick wall over there by the lookout and explode."

She pointed to the far side of Bluff Street, at the entrance to the Riverside Park Lookout. A ten-foot high brick wall separated the street from the scenic overlook, but another wall—made of wood painted to look like bricks, and backed by sandbags—had been put up in front of it. I guessed it was there to keep Brett from going into the brick wall in case something went wrong. Still . . .

"Sounds dangerous," I said. "I'm surprised Brett's doing his own driving."

"He's so brave!" Bess gushed. "I read how he always does his own stunts—he jumped off a ten-story building once! Into a net, of course, but still . . ."

Bess and I got out, heading for the extras' holding area, and George drove over to where Tina was standing, to check in.

Sylvia Trout was reading the *River Heights Bugle*. I

could see the front page, which featured a large photo of Brett Harley, locked in a tight lip-lock with some redheaded floozie.

Gulp.

The caption said, "Brett and Fiona heat up River Heights!" But I knew better. The girl in the photo was me—and the photographer was my soon-to-be-ex-boyfriend. Soon, as in the minute Dierdre decided to tell him about my dinner with Gordon MacIntyre.

"All right, extras," Tina said, approaching our holding area. "You'll be pedestrians, and you're going to be placed at intervals all along the street. As the speeding cars go by, you'll stop and point, or gasp, or whatever, until you hear Mr. MacIntyre say cut. Understood?"

I was not involved in the scene. Fiona's part called for her to run to Brett's car just after he did the turn, get in, and drive off with him. I saw that she had positioned herself to the left of the retaining wall, just barely out of camera range.

Glad to be left on my own, I got myself a hot cup of coffee and a doughnut, found a good perch for watching, and settled in for a nice relaxing morning.

I watched as Sebastian rigged the stunt car with explosive charges. Some were small patches he placed on the insides of the windshields. When they went off, these would look like bullets hitting the car. Then he put some on the inside of the door panels and the door of the trunk.

He wired the whole thing to a receiver, then disappeared under the car to fasten it on. I knew it would receive signals sent from a transmitter—probably connected to some computer program for precision timing.

Gordon supervised the whole thing, pacing nervously and making sure the charges were placed just right. He was really giving Sebastian a hard time, but I could understand why. After nearly getting his eyebrows singed off the other day, our director had the right to be a little testy.

Meanwhile the extras' cars began lining up all along Bluff Street and the steep hill of Sutter Avenue that dropped down from the hill above, ending at the overlook and the cement retaining wall that had been built in front of it.

I spotted George's old jalopy on Bluff Street, about fifty feet from the intersection. From her position, she'd have a perfect view of the whole scene. Much better than mine.

Which gave me a great idea . . .

First making sure that neither Tina nor Sylvia was looking, I went over to George's car. "Can I sit with you?" I asked. "They don't need me till the next setup, when Fiona does her part."

"Okay by me," George said. "Nice to have company."

The stunt car was ready, and now, it was moved onto a trailer and hauled up the hill for the start of the shot. Gordon hopped up there to give it one last look.

"I have a bad feeling about this shot," I told George.

"What do you mean?"

"I dunno. Just my sixth sense."

"You mean your crime feelers are tingling?"

"Yup." I tapped my toes, drummed my fingers on the dash, and watched as Gordon hopped off the trailer and it started up Sutter Avenue.

"Won't be long now," George said.

Gordon directed the cars to move in sequence. When he came up to ours, he told George, "You'll hear me say 'Car number three, go.' That's your cue. Go up to the edge of the intersection, and hit the brakes hard."

"Got it," George said.

"Hello, Nancy," he said, seeing me sitting there.

"Hi," I said.

There was something in his tone, and in mine, that caught George's attention.

"What was that all about?" she asked after he'd left.

"What was *what* about?"

She frowned, then sighed. "Nothing. I just thought for a minute there—never mind."

"Whatever," I said, glad she'd let it drop.

"Rehearsal!" Gordon's voice reached us through the megaphone he was holding. "And action! Car one, go . . . Car two, go . . . And Brett's car is coming down the hill, down the hill . . . and car three, go!"

George hit the gas, and three seconds later, slammed on the brakes. Good thing we were both buckled in.

The jalopy stalled, but luckily, George got it started again. "This cannot be good for my baby," she said, meaning the car. "Let's hope they don't do too many takes."

"I think they can only do one," I said. "Unless they've got another stunt car waiting—this one's going to be pretty messed up later."

"Okay, let's do it for real! Everybody back to one," Gordon announced. All the extras, including Bess, who was stationed near the retaining wall, went back to their original positions.

"This time it's for the money! And camera rolling . . . and . . . action! Go, Brett . . . Go, trailing cars . . . Car one, go . . . Car two . . ."

From my front-row seat, I saw Brett's Ferrari speeding down the hill, swerving back and forth to avoid the "bullets" being fired by the two trailing cars. This maneuvering of his caused the bad guys to collide two-thirds of the way down. This part had been carefully planned, with a second camera unit perched at that spot to catch the close-up.

With the bad guys out of the way, Brett, who was nearing the bottom, was supposed to hit the brakes and go into his spinning turn. I saw his car pass the designated spot—and continue without slowing down. I could even see Brett's face—the horrified look in his eyes . . .

And I knew he had no brakes.

"Car three . . . go!"

George hit the accelerator. Before she could hit the brakes, I said, "George, he's out of control—keep going!"

"*What?*"

"Keep going!"

Apparently Brett had no steering either. Instead of turning, he was heading straight for the ten-foot high cement wall—and Bess and Fiona, who were standing right in front of it!

10

Crash!

Seeing that George was frozen with confusion, I reached my foot over to the pedal and hit the gas, hard. We jerked forward with a screech of our wheels, just as Brett was barreling across Bluff Street toward disaster.

We hit his rear fender hard—so hard that it sent us into a spin very much like the one Brett was supposed to do. Luckily we didn't slam into anything or anyone else. We came to a stop right in the middle of Bluff Street.

"Are you okay?" I asked George, who was still wearing the same paralyzed expression on her face.

"I . . . think so," she said. "But my car!" She opened the door and got out, and I did the same on my side.

The car was obviously a total loss—the whole

front fender and hood were completely trashed. But never mind, I thought. George's car was headed for the junk heap anyway in the not-too-distant future. At least she'd put the old jalopy to good use one last time.

I wasted no more than five seconds inspecting the damage. George was clearly all right, so was I, and that was all that mattered on our end.

Next I looked around for Brett's car—and saw that it had been bumped to the right, where it had slammed into a pile of plastic containers that had been stacked along the curb. The containers were used to stow lighting equipment and scaffolding.

Brett's car had sent them flying, but thankfully, no one had been standing in that spot. Off to the left of the crash site, where Brett would have hit if we hadn't intervened, Bess, Fiona, and the crowd of extras they'd been standing with were all alive and uninjured, thank goodness—although most of them were now screaming Brett's name at the top of their lungs.

Everyone was running toward his car. Only Bess stopped to see if George and I were okay. I saw some production assistants reaching in and pulling Brett out of the smoking wreck. He was conscious, and I didn't see any blood, but he seemed kind of wobbly on his feet.

"What happened?" I heard him asking as he reached for the back of his head. "Ow—somebody conked me on the noggin!"

"You were in a crash, Brett," Gordon told him. Then, looking up at Tina, he barked, "Don't just stand there—go get an ambulance!"

Tina looked stunned, humiliated even. But she didn't argue. Instead she quickly turned and yelled at a lowly production assistant to do exactly what Gordon had told her to do.

They laid Brett down on the ground to wait for the ambulance, while Sylvia and Tina got busy herding the crowd away from the scene. In moments the sirens of the River Heights Ambulance Squad could be heard approaching. "Take him to the hospital and have him checked out," Gordon ordered. "We've got to get on with this shoot."

There was a murmur from the crew, who were obviously as shocked as I was that Gordon actually wanted to keep shooting after what had just happened. But I understood where he was coming from. Once it got out that there'd been another accident on the set of one of his movies, the studio might quickly shut things down. Gordon wanted—no, *needed*—to finish the shoot before the studio or the insurance people stepped in to stop him.

The ambulance pulled away with Brett inside.

Fiona made a huge fuss, demanding to go with him. Clearly the shock of the near-fatal accident had cleared her mind and focused it on how much she really cared for him. At least that's how I read her actions.

As the crew got busy cleaning things up, and a second Ferrari was rolled in for the getaway shot, Gordon finally got around to me and George. "Are you two all right?" he asked, coming up to the ruined pile of metal that had been George's jalopy.

"We're fine," George said, "which is more than I can say for my car."

"Well, don't worry," he told her. "The studio will reimburse you, I'm sure. Tina can get you a requisition form. And as soon as the police get here, you can file a report with them as well."

No sooner had he said the words than I saw a police detail coming toward us, having finished examining Brett's car. Chief McGinnis was with them, and he was not in a jolly mood. "How in the world could such a thing happen?" he was asking his lieutenants. "Didn't we have men posted all up and down the street?"

"Uh, yessir," said one of his men. "But nobody saw it coming. After all, it was just a vehicle malfunction."

"We'll see about that," the chief said. "Have it towed to the pound, and we'll get some experts in to look it over."

Off to one side, I saw a group of extras, including Bess and Dierdre. They all seemed eager to hear what the chief had to say about the accident.

"And who do we have here?" said the chief, seeing me standing there. "Why is it that whenever something goes wrong in this town, you're always right in the middle of it?"

"I happen to be an extra in the movie, remember?" I told him. "In fact, I'm Fiona Gibson's stand-in."

"Right," he said, his bushy dark eyebrows coming together in a scowl. "And I'm Santa Claus."

"It's true, Chief," George interrupted. "Nancy *is* Fiona's stand-in."

"I suppose these two are in the movie too," the chief said, indicating Bess and George.

"That's right, Chief," Bess said proudly. "I'm an extra, and so is George here."

He growled, and muttered something under his breath. "All right," he said, his face red as a beet. "Tow this hunk of tin to the pound as well. As for the three of you," he added, "come with me. You're going to file a report on this matter, and no one's free to go until I say so."

We spent the next two hours at the police station, giving him every detail of what had happened.

"I'm going to have a little word with the mayor about all this," Chief McGinnis said with a growl. "It may be good money for the town, but if she keeps bringing these crazy Hollywood types in here, I'm taking early retirement. It's just not worth all the stress."

He finally let us leave. We got back to the set to find that lunch was being served in Riverside Park. While we were eating, Gordon came back over to speak to me and George. "I don't know if I remembered to thank you both," he said. "Your quick reaction saved Brett's life—and probably some other people's as well, including Fiona's."

"It was Nancy who hit the gas," George said. "I was too stunned to move."

"Is that true?" Gordon said, training his amazing eyes on me.

"Well," I said, "I just couldn't let him slam into that wall with all those people standing in front of it. I mean, I could see that he had no brakes and no steering—"

"You're a hero, Nancy," he interruped me, taking both my hands into his. "Thank you from the bottom of my heart." He leaned forward and kissed me on the cheek, which to my mind was a bit much, especially in front of George.

"Oh, listen—the paparazzi will be wanting to talk to you about this," he added. "You might want to leave out that last part—about the brakes and steering—until the police have finished their investigation. You know . . . it might look bad for the film."

And for you, I thought, but didn't argue with him.

"I think I'd better go talk to the press," he said. "Don't go anywhere, Nancy—I'm going to want to shoot Fiona's close-ups right after lunch."

I saw Bess hurrying our way, holding a full plate of food and a can of soda. "Hi!" she said to Gordon. "I'm Bess Marvin, pleased to meet you! I'm a huge fan of your movies!"

"Pleased to meet you, too," he replied. "Now, if you'll excuse me . . ." He got out of there in a hurry. I was sure he'd been accosted by thousands of fans in his day.

"Did I say something wrong?" Bess asked us after he'd gone.

"Bess, it's not always about *you*," George said.

"Gordon's got his troubles right now," I added.

"*Gordon?* So it's true what Dierdre said!"

"Bess, you need to chill," I said. "I mean, a bunch of people almost just died—including you—or did that escape your notice?"

"You're the one who needs to chill, Nan," she said.

Then, "Dierdre told me about your dinner with Gordon. Were you going to keep it a secret forever?"

"What?" George said, her eyes widening in amazement.

"I was going to tell you both, of course," I said, fudging as best I could. "But it's not what you think."

"Oh, really? I suppose you're going to tell us you're working on a case now."

What could I say? "Bess, I promise, as soon as the shoot is done, I'll tell you everything—*everything*."

"Hmph. There'd better be a good reason you've been holding out on us," she said. Then she took a long look at George's car as it was being towed away to the pound. "Ooo. That's gonna need some bodywork."

"Destination: Junkyard," George said. "I only hope they give me a couple hundred for it."

Tina called my name over the loudspeaker, and I said good-bye to my friends for the moment. After an hour of posing in Fiona's place, she finally arrived on the set, back from River Heights General.

"Brett's fine," she said with a sigh of relief. "At least, he's telling everyone at the hospital that he has to get back here. They're not letting him go anywhere, of course. He's got to stay overnight for observation, but he'll be back for the grand finale tomorrow, the darling."

So much for their big fight. I guessed she wasn't holding it against him that he'd almost driven his car right into her. Her concern for her "poor baby" was obvious—so obvious that I wondered if it was a little overdone.

I looked up the hill, and saw Gordon coming back down Sutter Avenue, toward the set. I knew Sidney would be up there with the other paparazzi. Ned would be with them too—and I needed to talk to him, before this mess got any worse.

As I approached the roped-off area where the press was corralled, a hundred camera shutters clicked, over and over again. Sidney was there, all right, but there was no chance of us talking in the middle of this crowd.

I spotted Ned behind most of the others, wearing a glum look on his face. "Ned!" I shouted and waved, letting him know I wanted to talk to him.

But he just turned away and pretended he didn't see me. I tried to shove my way through the crowd, but by the time I did, he was gone.

I wondered if he'd ever forgive me. I thought he would—I mean, Ned has always been so reasonable. But then again, I'd never really put him through this kind of torture before.

I caught sight of him walking quickly away down Elm Street, and ran after him, grabbing him by the arm. "Would you please stop running from me?" I said.

He turned and stared hard at me, unyielding. "I've been doing a little research on Brett Harley," he said. "Turns out he's a real womanizer, Nan. I'd be careful if I were you—he might break your heart."

"You're the one who's breaking my heart!" I told him. "I don't care a thing for Brett! He took me totally by surprise when he kissed me like that—I just . . . I just didn't know how to react."

"Uh-huh. I'd say you reacted pretty instinctively."

"Ned—"

But he had already yanked his arm from my hand and was jogging off down the street.

"So, Ned's back on the market," came a familiar, grating voice in my ear.

"Dierdre!" I said. "You little sneak. Were you spying on our conversation?"

"You know," she said, "I've always had my eye on Ned. Now that he's available, I think I'll just make my move."

"He's *not* available!"

"Oh, isn't he?" She gave me her nastiest smile, then sashayed down Elm Street, following my boyfriend with nothing but evil intentions in her mind.

I could have killed her. Well, not killed her, but—Oh, you know what I mean.

I gave up for the moment and called his cell instead. The voicemail answered, and I left this message: "Ned, please let me explain. I really, really care about you, and there's nobody else in my life, I swear it. I can explain everything, if you'll just give me a chance. Please. Call me."

Then I hoofed it back down Elm Street, all the way to River Heights General Hospital. I was still working on a case, after all. I needed to see Brett Harley, and to confirm my growing suspicions about the accident.

The lobby was full of security people, and I had a really hard time getting through. Luckily one of them was an old classmate of mine, Matt Clayton, who used to have a crush on me way back before I started dating Ned.

"Ah, Nancy," he said, giving me a smile. "Digging up some celebrity dirt? Well, go on in, but don't stay too long—I don't want to get in any trouble for letting you by."

Brett was in the luxurious presidential suite, where Richard Nixon had once stayed after a bout of something intestinal. Brett was propped up in bed, watching a TV news report about the accident. When he saw me come in, he clicked it off, and took the ice pack off his forehead.

"Hey, there, gorgeous!" he said, giving me his best movie-star smile. "Come sit right here." He patted to a spot on the bed next to him.

"Thanks, I'll just stand," I said, noticing the red lump that was only half-hidden by his hair. "I can't stay long. I just wanted to check on a few things. . . ."

"Aw," he said, pretending to be disappointed. "Too bad."

"I happened to be right near your car when everything went wrong," I said. "I saw the look in your eyes."

"You mean that look of sheer terror?" he joked. "Yeah, I was pretty shocked when I hit the brakes and nothing happened. And then again when I tried to steer, and that was dead too."

"Any idea what went wrong?"

"Well, I'm no mechanic, but I did hear a kind of popping noise just before I realized I had a problem. I guess some cables just snapped all of a sudden."

I didn't say it, but I was thinking that things on cars don't just pop—not all by themselves, anyway. I remembered Sebastian under the car, placing his timers. He was looking more and more like my number one suspect.

"Why are you so interested, anyway? I thought you were an actress."

"Ha! Far from it," I said. "I'm more interested in criminal justice, actually."

"Ah, an amateur detective!" he said, rubbing the bump on his head. "Ow. Babe, you think you could get me some more ice? The stuff in this pack's melted."

"Sure," I said, and played nurse for a minute. Then, "Brett, tell me about Angelica. Do you think she could be the one behind the threats?"

"Possibly. But why would she be upset about the movie? She's the one who quit without warning. She can hardly blame Gordon for casting Fiona in her place."

"But say for a minute she did . . . Do you think she could have, well, sabotaged your car today?"

He laughed. "Now you *sound* like Fiona, too. No, that's a ridiculous idea."

"Why's that?"

"Because for one thing, she wasn't there—nobody's seen her for weeks or even knows where she is."

"She could be hiding out close by—even in disguise. I mean, she is an actress, after all."

"When you're a star, babe, it's impossible to hide. Ask any paparazzo. It's amazing she's stayed out of view for this long. But if she did come around the set, the whole world would know it. Besides, Angelica knows nothing about cars—I mean *nothing.* There's no way she could have cut my brake and steering cables. No way."

I could see his point. I could also see that the sun was setting over the river. Soon it would be dark—time for my next move.

"One more thing before I go," I said.

"For you, Sherlock? Anything." He reached for my hand, drew it to his lips, and kissed it.

"I wondered," I said, drawing something out of my purse, "if you could do me one, teeny, tiny little favor . . . ?"

11

Death in the Darkness

The River Heights Auto Impoundment Yard, or "the pound," as everyone calls it, lies north of town, in the old industrial district next to the ruined anvil works. During the day, it's a sea of trucks, cranes, and factory noise. But after dark it's as deserted as the wilderness, which is what I was counting on.

I'd heard Chief McGinnis say they were going to call in experts to examine the wreck of Brett's car "first thing tomorrow morning." That was typical of the speed he usually moved at—and it also reflected the reality that there were no experts in the field of car sabotage any nearer than the county seat of Silver Creek, fifty miles away.

I arrived just before dark, taking care to park my hybrid a couple blocks away, out of sight. I walked the rest of the way, and a good thing, too, because there at the front gate of the pound was Chief McGinnis himself, along with Officers Joe Rees and Emily Kim, both of whom I knew well from previous cases I'd been involved in.

I could see them, but since I was hidden behind a factory wall, they couldn't see me. All I had to do now was wait for them to leave. Of course, they might just decide to stay the night, in which case I'd have to come up with a Plan B.

After an hour they were still there. A cruiser pulled up and Officer Jeff Carr got out with a bag of doughnuts and a half-dozen coffees. Great. *Now* what was I going to do?

I decided to confront the situation head-on. Leaving my hiding place, I walked casually down the street, along the chain-link fence with its barbed-wire topping. "Hello, everybody," I said cheerily. "How's it going?"

"Well, if it isn't Little Miss Snoop," Chief McGinnis said, frowning so that his dark, bushy eyebrows met above his nose. "I'll thank you to steer clear of this investigation, missy. This is no place for an amateur."

Amateur! He knew how much it galled me to be referred to that way.

"I just thought I'd see what you guys found out about the car," I said.

"That's none of your beeswax," he replied, but out of the corner of my eye, I saw my buddy Officer Rees shake his head, telling me they hadn't found anything yet.

"You're so right, Chief," I said. "So, when's the expert arriving from Silver Creek?"

"Tomorrow first thing, if you must know," he said. "Don't you worry your little head about it, all right? Go back to playing movie star, and leave the investigating to the professionals."

I smiled, but didn't give him the satisfaction of an answer. "Well, I'll be going, then," I said.

"You do that—and give my regards to your dad," said the chief.

I kept on walking, until I was safely around the next corner. It was good and dark now, and I thought of scaling the fence, using the handy-dandy pair of wire cutters I always kept in the trunk of my car to clip my way through the fence. But no sooner had I disappeared from their view than the chief and his men got into their cruiser and disappeared.

"So, you think it's that easy to get rid of me?" I muttered under my breath. "No way, José." I went back to the gate, fished my lock-pick out of my fanny pack, and jimmied the lock. I swung open the gate, passed through into the pound, and closed it behind me, leaving it unlocked in case I needed to make a quick getaway.

The pound was an enormous open parking lot, about half-filled with cars in all states of repair. Some had been towed for being parked illegally. Others had been wrecked and abandoned in sundry out-of-the-way places and brought here to be examined and identified before being crushed into small cubes of steel.

The cars were parked in rows that led back into the semidarkness. I say *semi* because there were lights surrounding the pound. It's just that they weren't very bright—and why should they be? No one ever came here after dark—no one except me, that is.

I finally located Brett's car. It was parked at the very back of the pound, next to the fence, beyond which was a patch of litter-strewn woods. I noticed that someone had cut a small hole in the fence nearby, and wondered how long it had gone unnoticed.

Taking out my miniflashlight, I started examining the car. The hood had been folded nearly in two by the crash, so that it was easy to see underneath to the engine. There were still wires hanging where Sebastian had strung his minichargers, although the windshields, both back and front, were gone.

Kicking away the bits of shattered glass that littered

the ground, I got down on my back and edged my way under the chassis to get a better look.

There were the brake cables. They'd been severed, all right, but not by cutters, which would have left a clean edge. These cables had been blown apart by minicharges of the kind Sebastian had been placing on the windshields.

There were pieces of wiring, leading from the cables to the receiver and also to a well-hidden spot behind the transmission. There, I saw a charred area where a small extra detonator must have been placed.

I wondered if Chief McGinnis had noticed. Most likely not, I thought. What the chief knew about explosives, you could fit inside a vial of nitroglycerin.

I flashed back to my conversation with Sebastian Wright and tried to match the friendly, goofy-looking, bearded guy who'd been so willing to show me his handiwork with the would-be killer who'd done this to Brett's car. I couldn't help feeling that it didn't add up, but I couldn't think how anyone else could have done it.

I checked the steering cables and was not surprised to see that they'd been severed the same way. I was just about to shove my way out from under the car to get out of there before anyone found me when I felt a strong, powerful hand grabbing my left leg, and yanking me out!

"Well, if it isn't Nancy Drew—the new hero of River Heights!" said a familiar voice.

I shone a flashlight at his face. "Sidney! What are you doing here?"

"Isn't it obvious?" he said. "I'm a reporter, remember? Reporters investigate suspicious accidents. The question is, what are *you* doing here?"

I tried to think of a believable explanation other than the truth, but I came up empty. "I'll tell you, if you'll give me some info in return."

"Deal," he said. "You first."

"All right," I said, getting up and dusting myself off. "But I'd better not see anything about it in the papers. I'm a detective—sort of. I mean, I've solved quite a few cases in my time, although I've never actually been paid for it."

"A detective, eh? Well, that explains why you've been so nosy from the git-go."

"Yeah, well, I heard there'd been threatening e-mails, so I thought I'd get myself into the picture so I could investigate."

"Good thing you did," he said, "or Brett and Fiona would both be dead by now—along with two or three innocent extras."

"Thanks," I said.

"So what did you find under there, Sherlock?"

"Off the record?"

"Cross my heart," he said. I sure hoped he was as good as his word, but I doubted it.

"I found evidence of foul play," I said, leaving out the details about the explosive charges.

"Interesting," he said, "but not surprising. I suspected it from the moment the car went out of control. See, I'd heard about the letter Fiona got. Hadn't heard about the e-mails, though—thanks for that bit of info. Who received them, by the way?"

"Gordon and Brett."

"Hmm . . . sounds like someone's trying to stop this shoot any way they can." He smiled, exposing those awful teeth of his. "And I think I know who might be behind it."

"Angelica?"

"Oh, no you don't—you can read about it in the paper, just like everyone else. Boy, oh boy, this is gonna make me famous!" He rubbed his hands together excitedly. "Well, I'll be seeing you, Sherlock—and congrats again. Wait till you see the write-up I give you for saving all those people!"

"Hey, wait a second," I said, grabbing his arm before he could make his escape. "You owe me one, remember?"

"Okay," he said. "How's this—the cops had the

note to Fiona analyzed for prints, and guess what? They found a match, from a previous well-known shoplifting arrest."

"Angelica?" I guessed, vaguely recalling reading about it a few years back.

He smiled. "That's right. But it wasn't she who sabotaged the car."

Funny, that's exactly what Brett had said . . .

"How do you know? And if she didn't, who did?"

"Uh, uh, uh," he said, wagging his finger at me. "First you've gotta give me something else. Fair's fair."

At the moment I had nothing else left to give him—at least, nothing I was willing to have end up in print.

"No? Well, then, I'll be seeing you, kid." He yanked his arm free, and disappeared through the cut in the fence and into the darkness of the woods beyond.

As for me, I'd found what I was looking for. Now, I had to go find Sebastian. I knew he was staying at the Metropole, along with the rest of the cast and crew. I figured a late-night visit was appropriate, given the circumstances. So I started back for the main gate.

That's when I heard the noise. It was muffled, but definitely human—female, unless I missed my guess. And it seemed to be coming from a large Dumpster on my right, next to the fence by the side of the pound.

As I inched closer to it, the sound grew louder, but it was still muffled. Someone was definitely inside that Dumpster!

I hoisted myself up over the edge to get a better look—and there, bound, gagged, and lying on her back in the middle of a stinking pile of rotting garbage, was Dierdre Shannon!

"Why, Dierdre!" I said. "What are you doing here?"

"Mmgphgmfph!!" she said, her face reddening in anger.

I would have loved to stretch out this delicious moment, letting her go on and on without helping her. But of course I didn't—someone had tied Dierdre up and thrown her in here, and I needed to know who. So I hoisted myself over the edge and into the disgusting pile of who-knew-what and pulled the gag down out of her mouth.

"Nancy, you little witch!" she hissed. "Untie me, right this instant!"

"Not until you tell me who did this to you," I said.

"What do you mean?" she said, her eyes flashing fury. "*You* did it, of course! Who else?"

"*So* wrong," I said. "Why would I do a thing like that?"

"Duh, because you hate me! And because you know I'm gonna wind up with Ned Nickerson—and because I figured out that you're snooping around, investigating something to do with the movie—and because I followed you here, figuring you were up to no good."

"Well, I can't argue with any of that," I said, "except for the part about you winding up with Ned."

"What do you care?" she asked. "You're with Gordon MacIntyre, you lucky freak."

"I'm not, either, but never mind. I didn't do this to you, so who did?"

"I didn't exactly see anything," she said. "I mean, I was sneaking up on you, between the rows of cars, and somebody conked me on the head. Next thing I knew, I woke up bound and gagged. Speaking of which, would you mind setting me free?"

"Say *please*."

"Grrrr. Please!"

I lifted her up, and was starting to undo the duct tape that bound her wrists behind her back, when I thought I heard something. I stopped what I was doing to listen.

"What are you waiting for?" Dierdre asked.

"Shh!"

"Don't tell me to—"

Before she could say anything else, I put the gag back in place. "*Listen!*"

I could hear men's voices in the distance, arguing. Then there was a horrible, crunching sound, and after that, nothing.

I looked at Dierdre, who was staring at me with terrified eyes. I put a hand on her shoulder to calm her down.

We both heard footsteps, getting nearer and nearer until they stopped right outside the Dumpster. I held my breath, and even Dierdre was totally silent. The next thing we knew, something was hoisted up over the edge and fell into the pile of garbage next to us with a heavy thud.

It was Sidney—and I could tell by the vacant stare in his eyes that he was stone-cold dead!

12

Hot on the Trail

I heard footsteps running away at top speed. It was all I could do not to scream, and I wondered why Dierdre wasn't screaming herself, until I turned toward her, and saw that she had fainted dead away.

Well, I had no time right now to help her. I hoisted myself over the edge of the Dumpster and took off after those footsteps. They led back toward the cut in the fence. I got there, went through it into the patch of woods, and stood stock still, listening.

There was an eerie silence all around me. Suddenly I thought I might have made a fatal mistake. But then I heard branches rustling up ahead. I started after the noise, but by the time I was halfway there, I heard a car motor start, a screech of wheels, and a roar of the engine as it sped away, its lights off.

By the time I reached the source of the sound, it was too late—the car was gone. I saw some tire tracks in the mud—big wide ones with especially deep treads. I filed the pattern away in my memory bank for later. Then, out of breath and exhausted, I trudged back to the pound and the Dumpster.

Dierdre was still out cold, but her pulse showed she was all right. I untied and ungagged her, and got out of there in a hurry, heading back to my car. She'd be all right now.

Safely inside my car, with the doors locked, I called the police. In my best phony voice, I told them about Dierdre and the body in the Dumpster. I knew the voice wouldn't fool Chief McGinnis, but I hoped that by the time he got around to me, I'd have solved the case myself.

Next I phoned George, waking her up.

"Hello?" she said in a muffled voice.

"George, are you okay?"

"Huh? Of course I am, Nan. Why?"

"Did you go out with Sebastian tonight?"

"Well, sort of. I mean, he never showed up. I got tired of waiting after a while. How rude, huh?"

"I'm afraid it might be more than that," I said, and proceeded to tell her everything—about my investigation, the threats, and what happened now—Sid's murder and my suspicions about Sebastian.

"Oh, no—no way he killed anyone," George said, sounding wide awake now. "Not Sebastian. He may have stood me up, but he's still a pussycat."

"More like a jungle cat looking for a kill, if you ask me. I'm on my way to the Metropole right now," I told her, "to have it out with him before the police move in."

"Pick me up first, Nan—I'm coming with you."

"Sorry, George. This may get a little dicey, and I don't want to put you in danger."

"*You're* in danger, aren't you?"

"Well . . ."

"You *need* me there, Nan. Come and get me—*now*."

What could I say? "All right. I'll be there in five."

Together, George and I drove down to the Metropole and went inside. "You get the clerk away from the front desk for a minute," I told her, "and I'll take care of the rest."

George, who claims not to be an actress, could have won an Oscar for what she did next. "Please, help me!" she told the clerk, a fat, bushy-haired man of about fifty. "My friend is in the street, having a seizure or something!"

"I'll call the paramedics," said the clerk.

"No, no, I've already done that. I need someone to help me drag him out of the street!"

The clerk followed her out the front door. As

soon as they were gone, I ducked behind the desk and ran down the hotel register to find Sebastian's room. There it was—509. *Bingo.* I got back out from behind the desk just in time.

"I just don't understand it," George was telling the clerk as they came back through the revolving doors. "He must have gotten up and wandered off. . . ."

"I'm sure," said the clerk, frowning. "Next time, get someone else to help you."

"Sorry," she said, and followed me to the elevator bank around the corner of the hall.

We went up and found 509. I knocked, but there was no answer. Somehow I wasn't surprised. I fished out my lock pick, but I didn't need it—the door had been left unlocked.

The room had been trashed—whether by Sebastian or by someone else, it was impossible to say. "When was the last time you saw Sebastian?" I asked George.

"Right after the accident," she said. "He seemed totally freaked out—white as a sheet, in fact."

"Did he say anything to you?"

"Not about our date, if that's what you mean. But he did mention that he had to talk to Gordon about something right away."

"Hmmm. I wonder . . ."

We went back down to the lobby. "Go on ahead, George," I said. "I'll meet you outside."

I walked up to the clerk, and said, "Excuse me, I'm looking for a Mr. Sebastian Wright. He's supposed to meet me here, but I can't find him in his room. Did he leave any word for me—Nancy Drew?"

The clerk checked his notes. "Mr. Wright checked out earlier this evening," he said.

"Checked out? But—but that's impossible," I said. "Did he leave any word where he was going?"

"I'm sorry," said the clerk. "I have nothing here about that."

I went outside, and just as George and I got back in the car, her cell phone rang.

"Hello?" she said. "Sebastian! Where are you? What's happening?"

I put my ear close to hers, so I could hear his end of the conversation.

"Sorry I stood you up tonight, George," he said, "but I had to bug out. Somebody broke into my hotel room and trashed it—I guess they were looking for my keys, because they were gone from the drawer of my bedside table."

"Your car keys?" George asked.

"Yeah, and the keys to the truck where the pyro stuff is stored."

"What?"

"Yeah—my car was gone, but that's the least of it. Luckily I had another set of keys to the pyro truck, so I went back down to the set and checked. And it turns out that a whole bunch of stuff is missing! I . . . I don't know who to call. I tried to find Gordon, but he's off somewhere and I can't reach him by cell. He must have it turned off or something. Man, this is going to kill my career, between the car wreck and the missing explosives—"

I motioned for George to give me the phone. "Sebastian, this is Nancy here. I . . . I neglected to tell you, but I'm working on a case involving the film."

"Huh? Hey, what are you, a detective or something?"

"Yes. Sort of. Anyway, listen—what kind of car do you have?"

"It's an SUV."

"And the tires?"

"They're special off-road tires. I like to go off into the mountains with it on my off days . . ."

"Do they have really deep treads?"

"Yeah, why?"

"Really wide base?"

"Yeah . . ."

"Oh, boy."

"What? What's wrong?"

"Nothing—I'll tell you later. Listen, where are you now?"

"I'm—hold on . . ."

I looked at George and blew out a deep breath.

"Trouble?" she asked.

"Big time," I said.

"Hello?" Sebastian was back on the line.

"Yes, I'm here. Sebastian, do you think that someone might have used the stolen explosives to wreck Brett's car?"

"Definitely. But I don't think that's the end of it. Because there was a lot more missing than that."

"More explosives?"

"Explosives, detonators, timers—I'm telling you, it was enough to blow up a whole building and everyone in it. Man, I am totally up the creek!"

"Sebastian, you've got to tell the police, right away!"

"Yeah, I know, but—"

"And stay out of sight until I call you back, okay?"

"Listen, I've gotta go—someone's coming."

"Who? Who's coming?"

"I don't know, but I've gotta book. I'll call you la—"

"Sebastian, where are you? Sebastian?"

The phone suddenly went dead.

"What happened?" George asked, terror in her eyes.

"I don't know," I confessed. "But whatever it is, it's not good."

It was now after midnight. Case or not, I needed to sleep in the worst way. I dropped George off at home first. "Try to catch a few hours of shuteye," I told her. "He's probably okay."

"Probably?" She knew as well as I did that I was just trying to cheer her up. But what could we do in the middle of the night, with no idea where to look for Sebastian?

Before collapsing on my bed, I checked my phone messages. There were two—one from Tina, saying the call for tomorrow, the film's final day of shooting, was at three P.M. I was glad of that—it would give me the whole morning to track down Sidney's killer and find Sebastian.

The second message was from Ned, and it was much more troubling. "Nan, there's something I have to tell you, but it has to be in person. I'll see you at the set tomorrow, first thing. Nan, I . . . I'll talk to you then."

If I hadn't been so totally beat, it was the kind of message that would have kept me up all night.

I slept till eight, when I heard Hannah puttering around downstairs. "Hi, Hannah," I said sleepily, rubbing my eyes. "Is Dad around?"

"He's in the study, dear," she said. "Want some pancakes?"

"Mmmmm." Nothing's better than Hannah's pancakes. "I'll be right back for them." I went into the study, and there he was, just as advertised, going over some papers—for a case of his own, no doubt.

"Hi there, stranger," he said, a trace of concern in his voice. "How's it going?"

"Not so great," I admitted. I went on to tell him about Sidney's murder and my fears about Sebastian.

"You reported all this to the police, of course," he said.

"I called in to tell them about the body," I said.

"And the explosives?"

I bit my lip. I guessed I should have called that one in, too, but I just didn't trust Chief McGinnis to not mess things up.

"The chief isn't going to like this one bit," my dad said, picking up the phone. "And I want you to drop this case—*now*."

"Dad, wait a minute—I can't quit now. I'm right on the verge of solving the case, and I think I can nail Sidney's murderer if I have a few hours' lead time."

"Nancy, this is way too dangerous for you to go any further. Let the police handle it—it's their job, after all."

"I know, Dad, but—"

"No buts."

He punched in the number, and I left him to it. He had to do what he had to do—and so did I. Those explosives were out there somewhere, and I had to find them before it was too late.

13

The Fuse Is Lit

By the time I got down to the set, the police were all over the place. Chief McGinnis was in a heated argument with Gordon, who was insisting that the shoot had to go on.

"There's no way, sir," the chief said, his hands folded across his barrel chest. "We're officially on lockdown until our investigation is completed."

"You don't understand," Gordon said, "There are tens of millions of dollars at stake here—maybe hundreds of millions!"

"I can't help that," said the chief. "I've got my orders."

"Oh, yes? And who gives you your orders, may I ask?"

"I've got them straight from Mayor Simmons, sir."

"Well, let me talk to her then," Gordon insisted.

The chief scowled, but he took out his two-way radio and said, "Give me City Hall. Mayor Simmons's office." After a moment, he said, "Priscilla, it's Chief McGinnis. Let me speak to Her Honor, please."

"I'll talk to her," Gordon said, trying to grab the radio, but the chief wasn't having it.

"Hello? Hi there, Mayor. Chief McGinnis here. Mr. MacIntyre's insisting on going ahead with his film, ma'am. . . . Yes, I told him. . . . Yes, but he doesn't seem to—"

"Give me that!" Gordon said, snatching the radio right out of the chief's hands. "Mayor? Gordon MacIntyre here. Listen, I hope you understand what you're doing here—we're on a rigid schedule, and any delay will mean millions of dollars in losses, all of which the studio will be looking to recover from River Heights, plus punitive damages. . . . Yes, I understand, but this is the last day of filming. I don't see why the investigation can't wait till tomorrow. . . ."

He listened for another minute, then said, "Great. Thank you." Then he handed the radio back to Chief McGinnis. "Here," he said. "She wants to talk to you."

"Hello?" said the chief. There was a long silence,

and I saw his frown deepen, his bushy eyebrows coming together over his nose as his mood darkened. "I see. You understand, Mayor, that we have a dangerous criminal on the loose?" Another pause, then, "Yes, ma'am . . . whatever you say, ma'am—but I won't be held responsible if anyone else gets hurt."

He put the radio back in his belt and turned to Gordon. "I hope you're happy," he told him. "If anything else happens, it'll be your neck in the noose, not mine." He stormed off, followed by his men. "Ring this set with officers!" he shouted to them. "Nobody's to get through the cordon, I don't care who they are. Until this movie's finished shooting, nobody gets through without authorization!"

While all this was going on, Tina was organizing the extras for the afternoon's street shot. It was taking place on a stretch of Bradley Avenue, in the industrial section of town. The street was ringed by old factories and warehouses, some of which were abandoned and boarded up. One of them, I knew, would be used for tonight's inferno scene. But which one?

I needed to find out. And to do that, I had to get a look at the schematics for the scene. Those would have been on Sebastian's laptop computer. But with Sebastian gone, someone else would be in charge of rigging the pyrotechnics for the shot.

I wondered who . . .

I figured that my best chance of finding out would be to check Gordon MacIntyre's papers. Those would either be in Tina's hands or in his trailer. And since I stood zero chance of getting Tina to show them to me, I decided to have a look inside the trailer.

That wasn't as easy as it sounded. For one thing, I was on stand-in duty for the street scene for about an hour and a half. Then, when Fiona was supposed to show up to relieve me, she didn't.

Great. Someone else gone missing. Just what I needed.

"Somebody go get her," Gordon said, sighing in frustration. "Tina?"

"I'll go," I broke in before Tina could carry out his instructions. I knew Fiona's trailer was right next to Gordon's, and I figured this might be my best chance to get a look inside without anyone stopping me.

"Hurry up, Nora," Tina told me, getting my name wrong yet again. "We've got to get this scene shot before sunset."

"Right," I said, and took off jogging around the corner. I passed the extras' empty bus, then the costume trailer, and Brett's. He was just coming out the door as I passed.

"Nancy!" he said, taking me in his arms and hugging me. "How's my guardian angel?"

"Fine," I said. "I see you're feeling much better."

"Definitely," he said. "Thanks to you, babe. Listen, when this shoot is over, why don't I give you a call? We could go dancing—you know, to celebrate the film's wrapping and my miraculous survival."

"Um, I thought you and Fiona—"

"Ah, I've about had it with her," he said, waving his hand toward her trailer in frustration. "She's in there having a hissy fit, and I just can't take it anymore."

"I see," I said. "Well, I'm supposed to bring her down to the set."

"Right. Well, good luck—I couldn't get her to move. Maybe you can. Ciao, babe." He kissed me—on the lips, much to my surprise—and headed down the street toward the set.

I wiped my lips on my sleeve and looked around guiltily, just in case Ned was anywhere nearby, which thankfully he wasn't. Then I continued on to Fiona's trailer. Even from outside, I could hear her sobbing. I knocked—softly at first, then louder when she didn't answer.

"Who is it?"

"It's me, Nancy," I answered.

"Oh, good! Come in."

I did, and found her seated in front of her mirror, looking at herself and trying to wipe off the smeared mascara that marred her usual good looks.

"What's up?" I asked her. "They want you down on the set."

She sniffed back tears. "I know that."

"Well?"

"They can just bloody well wait," she said, tossing a tissue into the wastebasket and grabbing another. "I can't very well act looking like this, can I?"

"Um, would it be a stupid question to ask what the problem is?"

"Oh, Nancy," she said, and started bawling again. "I can't go on with this—I just can't! I just know Angelica's out there somewhere, waiting to take her revenge on me. She almost succeeded yesterday, and today's the last day of filming, so . . ."

"But it was Brett's car that was sabotaged," I pointed out.

"Yes, but he would have plowed right into me if that other car hadn't crashed into him! Don't you see? She planned the whole thing to kill both of us! And the other day, when Gordon almost got torched? I'm telling you, Nancy, she's after all three of us—and today's the day!"

"Look, is there anything I can do?" I asked.

She took both my hands in hers and clutched them for dear life. "Yes!" she said. "You can take over for me!"

"*What?*"

"It would be no problem, Nancy—I don't have any lines in these two scenes. I just scream, and run, and look scared, and most of the shots are from a distance. I'm sure Gordon can adjust to you doing it for me!"

I flashed back to something I'd read in one of those old *Hollywood Gazettes*—or was it Sidney who'd told me, or Ned . . . ? Anyway, it was that Fiona had backed out of doing that stunt on Gordon's last movie—the one where the stuntwoman died in her place.

Was I being set up to be the next victim?

I thought about it for a moment. If I refused, she would surely back out, and the film would be stopped in its tracks. Not that I cared about that so much, but my only chance to nab whoever killed Sidney and was planning more violence was if the shoot went forward.

"Okay—I'll do it," I said. "If Gordon's okay with it. But you'll have to convince him."

"Oh, Nancy!" She hugged me so tightly I thought I would faint. "You're a lifesaver."

I certainly hoped so—but that part was still very much in doubt.

"Let's go tell him right now," she said, grabbing me by the hand.

"Wait—you go," I said. "I'll wait here. I don't want to get involved in this. Just tell him it's okay with me."

"Fine," she said. After doing a quick fix on her face, she left me there, sitting in her trailer.

As soon as she was gone, I went back outside and continued on to Gordon's trailer. It was locked, naturally, but I've never let locked doors stop me before. With my trusty lock pick, I was inside within thirty seconds, closing the door behind me.

I didn't want to stay long—someone could come around at any moment, and if I was caught in there, my whole investigation would be endangered. So I started looking around for anything that would tell me about that night's pyrotechnic plans—a drawing, a schematic, a map—anything.

I opened drawers, notebooks, pored through piles of papers on his desk—nothing. Then I started going through his clothes, to see if there was anything in one of the pockets.

In his canvas jacket, I found what I was looking for. It was a drawing of a six-story warehouse, with marks where all the controlled fires and explosions were to occur. There was nothing to indicate which building it was, but I recognized the Hinckley Building facade, a former fabrics company that had gone bankrupt back in the 1970s—perfect for the period of the movie.

Now that I knew where to look, I replaced the drawing where I'd found it. It was time to go back to Fiona's trailer and wait for her return. I was almost out the door when something made me stop in my tracks.

I heard a cell phone ring.

There was a tiny bathroom in the trailer, and the door to it was open. On the sink, sitting there where he'd obviously forgotten it in his hurry to get to the set, was Gordon's BlackBerry. It was jumping around from the vibration of the ringing. Seeing that it was about to fall off the sink and possibly get damaged, I went to grab it—and that's when I noticed the caller ID.

It was a long, long number. That told me the call was coming from a foreign country. Acting on a hunch, I pressed the green button, and in my deepest, manliest, most Gordon MacIntyre-like voice, I said, "Yes?"

"Gordon? Is that you?"

I recognized the voice immediately, as anybody would have who'd seen any of her movies. The voice belonged to Angelica Reeves.

"Mm-hm," I said.

"I know you told me to stay put, but I'm getting nervous—when can I come back?"

My throat felt suddenly parched. I couldn't have answered her if I wanted to.

"Gordon? Are you still there? Gordon?"

I cut off the call, and put the BlackBerry down where I'd found it. My head was spinning suddenly. So it was Gordon who'd hustled Angelica out of the country!

But *why*? So she wouldn't disrupt the shoot?

But if it wasn't Angelica behind the e-mails and the note . . . and if it wasn't Sebastian, then . . .

I was almost to the door of the trailer when I heard someone coming up the steps on the other side of the door. Quickly I backed into the tiny closet and closed the door, leaving it open just a crack.

Tina entered the trailer, and started looking around for something. Not finding it on the desk, she checked the bathroom and found the BlackBerry. She grabbed it, stuck it in her pocket, and left as quickly as she'd come.

I figured that Gordon must have sent her here to get it. But how lucky had I been to be there at just the right moment!

I left the trailer and got back to Fiona's just before she returned. She didn't look happy.

"What did he say?" I asked.

"He said you could do the street scene for me, but tonight, it has to be me." She burst into tears and buried her face in my shoulder. "He told me I'd signed a contract, and if I backed out, he'd sue me for everything I was worth!" Sobs wracked her body, and I patted her gently, trying in vain to soothe her.

"I'd . . . I'd better get down to the set, if I'm going to be you for this shot," I said, breaking away from her. "You'll be okay, Fiona—don't worry, nothing's going to happen to you tonight."

"But . . . but how can you be sure?" she asked, sounding like a frightened little child.

"Trust me," I said. "Everything's going to be all right."

I wished I was as sure as I sounded, but really, it was all an act. My dad was right—I could really act with the best of them when lives were on the line.

It was already close to six, and there were only two hours of daylight left to get the street shot in. I was just on my way to the set when, passing the costume trailer, someone stepped out from behind it and blocked my way.

"Ned!"

"Nancy," he said, and I could see at once that his face was clouded with worry.

"Oh, Ned, I've been wanting to talk to you!"

"And I with you."

"But I can't right now—I've got to get to the set."

"This can't wait, Nan."

"It has to."

He grabbed me by the shoulders. "Nan, I heard about you and Gordon MacIntyre."

"Ned, please—there's nothing between me and Gordon. Dierdre's just out to break us up, don't you see? She wants to go out with you herself!"

"Nan, I wish I could believe that."

"Believe it! I swear it's true!"

"Just—just watch out for him," he said, looking sadly into my eyes.

"Huh?"

"I've . . . I've been doing some research," he said. "MacIntyre's last girlfriend was killed on the set of his last movie."

"His last . . . but I thought Fiona was his last girlfriend."

"Oh. Right. The one before her. She was Fiona's stand-in on the movie, and—"

"Wait," I said. "I thought the girl who died was a stuntwoman."

"No. It was her stand-in," he said. "Here—you can read the articles yourself."

He handed me a few sheets of paper, and left. I tucked them in my back pocket to read between scenes, and headed down to the set. The sun wasn't going to stand still in the sky, after all. There'd be time to read them later.

It was after sunset when I finally got a chance to look over the pages Ned had given me. They were not from *Hollywood Gazette*, but from some rag sheet called *Movietone*. I recognized the byline, though. The author was none other than the late Sidney Green.

The twists and turns of fate are stranger than any fiction could ever be. Gorgeous actress Madeline Grey, who died in a fall from a cliff during last week's filming accident on the set of the movie *Scimitar*, was recently spotted at a romantic hideaway with up-and-coming actor Brett Harley, who made such a splash in last year's *Kill Me Deadly*.

But as recently as two weeks before that, Ms. Grey had also been romantically linked with director Gordon MacIntyre. Rumor has it that Brett swept her off her feet, and that MacIntyre was furious over the betrayal.

Adding to the strange twists of fate, Grey was standing in for Fiona Gibson, star of *Scimitar*, who had for some strange reason refused to do the stunt on the cliff, even though she'd always done her own stunts before.

Could it possibly be that the terrible "accident" that befell Ms. Grey was no accident at all? No wonder Wagner Pictures has terminated MacIntyre's five-picture contract, blaming him for the young woman's death. Perhaps Brett and Fiona should be worried about their own safety. In fact, Fiona may have been worried to distraction—this reporter tracked her down at *Tranquility Arms*, a well-known "recovery spa" for the emotionally fragile rich and famous, where she's been "taking the cure" ever since the tragic events of last month.

I couldn't believe what I was reading. Suddenly all the pieces began to fall into place—motive, opportunity, means—they were all there. There was only one thing that didn't make sense, and that was the explosion that had almost killed Gordon MacIntyre.

It was dark now, and I watched, following behind at a safe distance as Gordon and Tina led Brett and Fiona into the Hinckley Building. "We'll be on the top floor," he was explaining. "Cameras are both inside and out. When the fires are set off, you, Fiona, will call out the window for help. Brett, you'll rush in, run up the stairs, and grab her in your arms. Then we'll film you as you leave the building—and finally, the big explosions that would have incinerated you both if you hadn't been the heroes of the film."

He laughed, and clapped each of them on the back. "I hope you're both ready for the wrap party afterward," he said. "It's going to be a real blast—pardon the pun!"

I had been trying all evening to think things through. If I was right, and whoever had stolen the explosives from the pyro truck was planning to bring down the building, I figured they'd have planted the charges far from the actual shot, where they could do the most damage without being detected.

That would be the basement—which is where I was now headed.

I can't tell you how creepy it was going down those dusty, crumbling stairs in the near-total darkness, while rats and roaches scampered in every direction, scattering from the beam of my flashlight.

The Hinckley Building was a big one, and that meant there was a large area to search. But I was going on the premise that the killer wanted to bring down the entire building, along with everyone in it. So that meant he—and I was sure now that it was a he—would place the charges in the four corners of the building, as well as all along the supporting outer walls.

At the bottom of the stairs, I played my flashlight all around. Spiderwebs were everywhere, and the spiders in them were gigantic. But there was something else I found—footprints. Men's footprints, two sets of them. Someone had been here before me, and not too long ago, either.

The footprints went in different directions, which told me that he had made more than one trip down here. But there were two distinct, different patterns, and that surprised me. I'd thought I was dealing with only one culprit, but if there were two . . .

I worked my way as quickly as I could, considering that I had to push aside all those spiderwebs to get where I was going. The culprit would have had to brush them aside, too—but spiders are notoriously fast weavers, and they'd made their repairs quickly.

I got to the corner of the building, and there, flush against the steel beams, were several sticks of what looked like dynamite! Connected to them was a timer, blinking red at intervals of a few seconds.

I know very little about explosives, but I could tell two things just by looking at these—first, they were wirelessly connected, so there was nothing to clip. And second, I had no idea how to disable them.

I thought of the group upstairs, preparing to act out the final shot of the movie. In the script, everybody survives the fire and blast. But in real life, if these explosives went off, along with the others I was sure were placed in the other three corners of the basement, nobody was getting out of here alive.

"Why, if it isn't Nancy Drew."

I froze, then gasped in horror, turning quickly. There, with a pistol in his hand pointed straight between my eyes, was none other than Gordon MacIntyre!

14

The Walls Come Tumbling Down

"I'll thank you to drop that flashlight," he said, shielding those gorgeous eyes of his from the glare.

I did as he said. I'm not one to argue with a man pointing a gun at me.

"That's better. Now kick it over here."

He bent down slowly to pick it up in his free hand. "I *thought* there was something not quite right about you," he said. "Something just a little too curious for an ordinary young girl." He was just a silhouette now, and I had to squint even to see that. "Your chief of police is a very talkative fellow. When he told me you were an amateur detective, I realized I'd better pay close attention to you."

"I guess that explains the dinner invitation," I said bitterly.

"Up to a point," he says. "You are also quite attractive, so it wasn't exactly painful taking you to dinner."

"Thank you . . . I guess," I said.

"Such a pity," he said. "Such a waste of young talent. You would have made an excellent actress, you know."

"I'm flattered."

"Yes, well . . . I'm afraid I'm going to have to bind your hands and feet, my dear. I'll thank you to turn around now—no funny business, please. I'm a rather desperate man, as I'm sure you've figured out, judging by the fact that you're here in the basement."

I turned my face to the wall and put my hands behind my back, all the while trying to think my way out of this mess. He bound my hands with the same duct tape that he'd used on Dierdre at the pound. Then he made me sit down while he taped my ankles together.

"I'll spare you the gagging," he said in a kindly voice. "No one can hear you down here anyway, no matter how loudly you scream."

"I'm not much of a screamer," I told him.

"Good."

"Before you go," I said, "since I am so curious, as you said—would you mind telling me why?"

"Why I'm doing all this?" He sighed. "I'm sorry, but you know, time is money, and I'm in a race against the clock, as I'm sure you know—Chief Whatshis-name is quite anxious to get this over with, and in my own way, so am I."

I couldn't let him go yet, not until I figured out a way to save myself and the others. "You killed Sidney, didn't you? And wrote those threatening e-mails and the note to Fiona?"

"Of course I did."

"But I don't understand why! Why would you risk your own comeback movie being shut down before it was finished?"

"That's easy. I did it to get even."

"With who? And why?"

He chuckled softly. "It was a brilliant concept, I think you'll admit. I'm going to have my revenge on all my enemies and enjoy my greatest triumph at the same time. It may end up being my last film, but then, you never know. Life is long, and there's always a chance for another comeback when you've been as famous as I."

"I don't understand. Who are your enemies, and what did they do to you?"

Now an edge of anger tinged his voice. "First and foremost, there's the studio. It was their fault that I lost the one true love of my life."

"Madeline Grey?"

"Ah, you've done your homework—good for you.

Yes, Madeline. She would never have died if the studio hadn't pressed me so hard to wrap up shooting in a mere two weeks. It made my crew cut corners—so much so that an explosive charge was left in place to do its deadly work."

"And that pyro man . . ."

"Yes . . . I took care of him a couple of weeks ago. There are drugs you can get over the Internet these days . . . drugs that mimic the symptoms of a heart attack, and are untraceable after two hours have passed."

"And Sidney?"

"That worm? That slimy, disgusting excuse for a reporter? He trashed me in the papers, so much so that the studio wound up blaming me for Madeline's death! Me! Can you imagine? Me, who loved her more than anything on Earth! Believe me, the world is well rid of Sidney Green."

"And Brett? And Fiona?" I thought I knew the answer, but I needed to keep him here for as long as possible. As long as he was talking, everyone was safe. Once he left . . .

"Brett, ah yes . . . He stole Madeline's affection from me, and for that alone, he deserves to die. And Fiona? Ha! If she hadn't been such a diva, and begged off doing the shot, it would have been her who died, not Madeline. Now, they're both going to pay."

"And what about Angelica?" I asked. "What did she do to you?"

"She? Why, nothing. Nothing at all. She's a dear, sweet girl, who's been wronged by Brett and Fiona just as I have been. It's really too bad she's going to have to take the blame for all this."

"I don't understand. . . ."

"Don't you? I think you do, Nancy. You're such a bright girl. No?" He sighed. "All right—I haven't the time to play games with you, so I'll just tell you the short version. Angelica was dumped by Brett, and she was quite upset about it—especially when he took up with Fiona, as you can imagine. So when I contacted her, and sympathized—she was putty in my hands. You see, I am a director, and a great one at that. My gift is manipulating others and getting them to do my will. It was easy to lead her. She got me hired for this film, the darling girl. I knew she'd been stalking Brett and Fiona after they got together, and I know I can make her take the rap for all of this. I gave her careful instructions not to see or talk to anyone until I gave her the okay."

"You must have promised her something in return," I said. "Actresses don't walk out on starring roles without a good reason."

"Very perceptive!" he said. "Bravo. You know, for an amateur, you really are quite talented. Much quicker on the pickup than your bumbling police chief."

"Thank you," I said. "Go on. You were saying?"

"I promised Angelica that Fiona would soon be out of the picture. That was good enough for her. Of course, so will Brett—but she doesn't know that yet. I'm sure she thinks it's all going to be nonviolent, too. She's such a sweet girl . . . wouldn't really hurt a fly, passionate as she is."

"And the e-mail you sent yourself? And the explosion that first day of shooting that almost killed you?"

"Oh, hardly," he said, chuckling again. "Just a diversion, really. All the threats and that little bang were meant to throw suspicion off me, and make everyone think someone wanted to stop the shooting of my film. It made me look very much the victim, don't you think?"

"Yes . . . I certainly believed it for a while—until I found out that Madeline had been your girlfriend . . . and until Angelica called on your BlackBerry and I happened to pick it up."

"Ah! So that explains how you got onto me. You snuck into my trailer, didn't you?"

I admitted that I had.

"Naughty, naughty girl," he said. "I'm afraid you're going to have to be punished." He put the gun back in his pocket and backed away. "I'm afraid this is good-bye, Nancy. I'm so sorry—you really don't deserve such a horrible end. But then, as they say, 'that's show business.'"

And then, as quickly as he'd come, he was gone. I was alone in the dark, in the basement of a building that was about to come down on top of me.

I wracked my brain for a way out of this mess, but kept coming up empty. I thought of my dad . . . of Ned . . . of Hannah, and Bess, and George . . . They were all going to miss me terribly.

And then I heard footsteps again. Was Gordon coming back? Why would he?

The beam of a flashlight played all around, as if looking for something. "I'm over here!" I cried out. "In the corner!"

"Nancy? My gosh—what are you doing here?"

"Sebastian!"

Yes, it was good old Sebastian Wright, and he couldn't have picked a better moment to reappear.

"Where have you been?" I asked him.

"I had to disappear for a while—Gordon was after me, and he even took a few shots at me last night after I hung up with you and George. But what are *you* doing here?"

"I cracked the case and figured out that the building

was wired to blow, but Gordon found me here and tied me up—speaking of which . . ."

"Oh—sure . . ." He quickly cut me loose.

"And what are you doing here?" I asked. "How did you know to—"

"I'm afraid I've been holding out on you," he said. "I'm a private investigator based in Silver Creek. Also a former Special Forces guy with a specialty in explosives. Your dad hired me to keep an eye on the picture—"

"And on me," I finished for him.

"Well, yeah. Except I got myself in trouble, didn't I?"

"I'll say. Now how about disconnecting these explosives?"

He played his flashlight on them. "Uh-oh," he said. "This is not good . . . not good at all."

"Meaning?"

"I can't dismantle it—it's rigged to go off if it's interfered with."

"How in the world could Gordon know how to do that?" I asked.

"Hey, the Internet is amazing," he said. "You can learn anything in a hurry—especially bad stuff." He looked at me, and I saw the fear in his eyes. "What are we going to do now?"

I already knew the answer. "I'm going upstairs to

get everyone out of the building. You go find Gordon, and make sure he doesn't get anywhere near the detonator before we get out."

"I'll do my best," he said. We went up the stairs to the ground floor. Leaving me with the flashlight, he left the building by a side door so as not to be seen. Then I continued upstairs, running for all I was worth.

I burst onto the sixth floor to find Fiona, Brett, and two cameramen, along with Tina.

"We've got to get out of here—now!" I yelled.

Tina wheeled on me. "Shh!" she said. "We're about to shoot the scene!"

"No! We've got to go—the building's going to explode! Gordon's trying to kill us all!"

"Don't be ridiculous," she said. "He would never do that!"

But I saw that I'd struck a chord with Fiona. "I'm getting out of here," she said. "Better safe than sorry. Brett?"

He looked undecided, but when Fiona stamped her foot, he said, "Whatever you say, babycakes. Sorry, Tina. We can always come back up if it checks out safe."

Tina was already on her radio. "Gordon? We've got a problem here."

His voice came in over the static. "What's up, Tina? We're ready to roll down here."

"That girl Nora just showed up."

"Nora?"

"You know, the stand-in. She says you're trying to kill everyone. Isn't that crazy?"

There was a moment of silence before he answered. "Tina, we're rolling, in one . . . two . . ."

"Everybody run for the exits!" I shouted.

Fiona led the rush to the stairs, followed by Brett and the cameramen.

"Wait!" Tina shouted after them.

"Tina—believe me," I pleaded. "Your life is at stake. We need to go *now.*"

Something in my tone must have convinced her, because she came along with me to the stairs. "Tina? Are you there?" Gordon's voice came over the radio. "Camera rolling . . . and . . . action!"

I knew we had only seconds to get down the stairs and out. I don't think I've ever run that fast in my entire life. Below, I saw the others get to the stairwell and throw the door open.

"What's happening?" Gordon's voice crackled. "What the—oof!"

I hoped that sound was Sebastian tackling him before he hit the detonator. But I didn't wait to find out. Tina and I burst out of the building and onto the floodlit street. Across the way, I could see a fight going on with Gordon and Sebastian throwing punches at each other.

Finally Gordon burst free and reached fo
thing. Behind me, I heard a tremendous boom
the next thing I knew, I was thrown into the air a
forward, landing in a heap against the building across the way. There was a huge flash, tremendous heat, and looking up, I saw the Hinckley Building begin to fall.

"Everybody run!!" someone shouted, and everybody did.

Luckily it took about ten seconds before the building collapsed in a heap of smoke and fire. As the flames rose, I saw Chief McGinnis and his uniformed men racing toward us.

"Cut!" I heard Gordon shouting. "Great! That's a wrap!"

"Yes, it is," I said, coming up to him, and watching as he went white as a sheet at the sight of me. "A wrap to your criminal career." Turning to Chief McGinnis, I said, "Here's your man, Chief. I hope you've got your cuffs handy."

As he and his men took Gordon MacIntyre into custody, the chief turned to me and said, "I've got to hand it to you, Nancy. This time, you actually helped us solve a case—a little."

I could have killed him—but then, it didn't matter who got the credit. A criminal had been foiled and his intended victims mostly saved.

Me included.

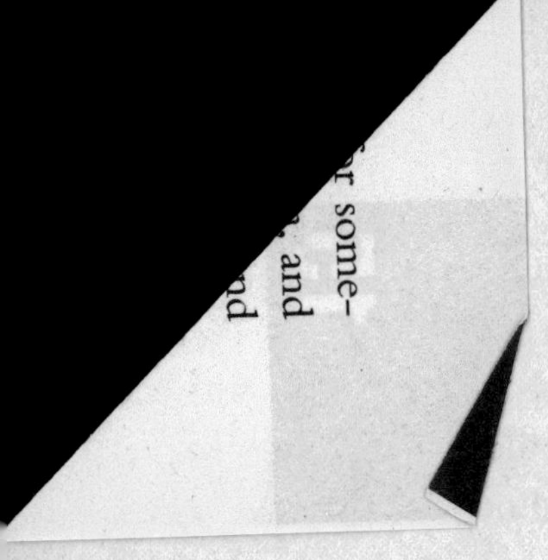

Happy Ending

"I can't believe I'm actually going to see myself in a movie!" Bess said, as she, George, and I took our seats for the invitation-only preview of *Love Me to Death* at the River Heights Multiplex Cinema. "This is the most exciting thing that's ever, ever happened to me!"

"Calm down, Bess," said George. "Just remember . . . it's only a movie."

Bess rolled her eyes. "Only a movie. Right. George, you're hopeless."

"Shh!" I said as the lights went down and the movie's hard-charging music came up.

"How did Gordon ever finish the movie?" Bess whispered to me. "I thought he went straight to prison after that night."

"He did," I told her. "I heard Tina was promoted to supervise the editing."

"Shh! Both of you!" George said. "Here we go!"

I knew she was as excited as the two of us, but George would never let it show. Still, as the movie unfolded and as the River Heights scenes flashed before us, everyone in the crowded, dark theater oohed and ahhed. There was Mason's Drugstore and Olde River Jewelers and Riverside Park. And there, in the street scenes, were familiar faces in the background.

I can't really tell you whether the movie was good or not, to be honest. Brett and Fiona were their usual, beautiful selves, of course. And the car-chase scene was awesome—especially when George's Lincoln rammed Brett's Ferrari and sent it spinning. It was strange to see it from afar, after having actually been in the car.

"This is so awesome!" Bess said. "Hey, there I am!"

"Where?" George said.

"You didn't see me? I was right there!"

"For how long? Half a second? I must have blinked."

"I'm telling you, I was there—wasn't I, Nan?"

"Uh, yeah," I said, although it really could have been anybody. Bess, or whoever, had just been a blurry face in the crowd near the brick wall at the lookout.

"Why don't you just chill, Bess?" It was Dierdre, leaning forward from the row behind us. "You were so far in the background in that scene, you were more like atmosphere."

"Why don't you just zip it, Dee Dee?" Bess shot back. "I don't remember having seen *you* yet. Have you, girls?"

"Don't worry," Dierdre said smugly. "My big scene is coming up."

I tried to spot Dierdre in the next scene, outside the burning warehouse, but I couldn't. I thought I'd just missed it somehow, till she stood up behind us, gasping.

"I can't believe this!" she said, loudly enough to draw shushing from the crowd. "They cut me out of the scene! This is an outrage—I'm going to complain to the studio!" She stormed up the aisle and straight out of the theater, no doubt on her way to tell Daddy she'd been treated unfairly by that awful Tina, who'd edited her right out of the picture.

To tell you the truth, I felt a little sorry for her. She'd worked hard, like the rest of us, and she'd endured getting conked on the head and tossed in a Dumpster full of rotting garbage simply because she was in the wrong place at the wrong time. She did deserve at least a moment of on-screen time.

"Hey, Nan," George asked, as the movie ended with a passionate, on-screen kiss that was all too familiar. "Isn't that you?"

It was me, all right—or rather, the back of my head as Brett laid a lip-lock on me.

"Nan, you're a star!" George whispered, elbowing me as the music swelled, the credits rolled, and the crowd applauded and stood up to go.

"Yeah, that's me," I said. "I think I'll quit show business while I'm ahead."

Bess sighed. "You really didn't see me, George?"

"Oh, Bess," George said, draping an arm around Bess's shoulder. "We'll go see it again when it opens, and you can point yourself out to me."

"Yeah! And Nan, you can bring Ned!"

"I don't think so," I said. "I think he'd like to forget the whole movie after all that happened."

"You're probably right," Bess agreed. "Still, it must have been awesome to kiss Brett like that. Was it awesome?"

"It was okay," I admitted. "Oh, that reminds me, Bess—I've got something for you." I fished in my bag for the souvenir I'd gotten from Brett at the hospital. "This is for you. I totally forgot I had it."

I handed her the piece of paper, and she read it out loud. "'To Bess . . . with all my love and affection,

Brett Harley'!" Bess's jaw dropped, and she shrieked so loud my ears hurt. "Oh Nancy! I love you! You are the best friend in the whole wide universe!"

Later that evening, I drove over to Ned's house and rang his doorbell. He answered it himself. "Hi there," I said. "Remember me?"

He tried to frown, but he couldn't help smiling. "I think so," he said. "Maybe you'd better remind me."

"I'm Nancy . . . your girlfriend?"

He looked skyward, torturing me. "It's . . . coming back to me . . ."

"Maybe this will help you remember," I said, and putting my palms on his cheeks, I kissed him.

"I can't believe my eyes!" came an annoyingly nasal voice from the street behind us. It was Dierdre, sitting in the front seat of her car. She'd obviously just driven up to the curb, with the intention of paying a call on Ned to see if he was available. "Ned, you forgave her after what she did to you?"

Ned put his arm around me and smiled. "I can't help it," he told her. "I have a thing for movie stars."

Then he kissed me again as Dierdre's tires screeched and her car roared off into the distance.